Doc Manners had said, "Weakfoot is big, and black and vicious. A killer cat. With the speed of greased lightning!"

Lonny dived to the ground and rolled to one side, pointing the rifle automatically. The deafening roar of the shot made his ears hum.

The panther jumped, twisted crazily and fell. At once it was on its feet again and Lonny's tongue went dry.

Weakfoot's glistening coat of blue-black hair was stained crimson.

For a moment boy and beast looked at each other . . .

THE GHOST
OF CRAMER'S
ISLAND

LINDA CLINE

Originally published as *Weakfoot*

BANTAM BOOKS · TORONTO · LONDON · NEW YORK

RLI: VLM 6 (VLR 5-7)
IL 6+

WEAKFOOT

*A Bantam Book | published by arrangement with
Lothrop, Lee & Shepard Company*

PRINTING HISTORY
*Lothrop, Lee edition published March 1975
Bantam edition | November 1976
2nd printing
3rd printing*

ISBN 0-553-02457-4

Published simultaneously in the United States and Canada

Bantam Books are published by Bantam Books, Inc. Its trade-
mark, consisting of the words "Bantam Books" and the por-
trayal of a bantam, is registered in the United States Patent
Office and in other countries. Marca Registrada. Bantam
Books, Inc., 666 Fifth Avenue, New York, New York 10019.

PRINTED IN THE UNITED STATES OF AMERICA

to
Susan Lois Palmer
and her mother
Susannah Gardiner Palmer

THE GHOST OF CRAMER'S ISLAND

Prologue

I met the old man by accident. I had arrived by getting lost. His home was a shack, weatherworn, unpainted; there was no running water or electricity. He said he had never been out of the county but once and that was a trip of less than a hundred miles. When he was young, there had been no automobiles, nor any paved roads. No airplanes had ever crossed the skies.

His home was four miles off Highway 177, eleven miles from Edith, Georgia. I had driven down a narrow, twisting sandy road, which ended in his packed clay yard. It is an area we know today as the great Okefenokee Swamp. But to the old man and the people in his story, it was "Cypress Swamp." He told these events as truth.

I repeat the story, as I heard it, as he told it to me.

1

1

Bay's nose quivered and his long tail wagged slowly back and forth. Lonny Bascombe hooked a cow horn on his belt, aware of the redbone hound's eyes following every movement. Pa and Aunt Louise watched the boy and his dog, Pa's blue eyes twinkling. Bay did a side-walking dance as Lonny lifted the long-barrelled rifle down from two pegs on the wall. Pa had built the gun rack for the boy when Lonny received the rifle last year. Lonny pulled back the single hammer and pretended to examine the weapon closely. A throaty grumble rose from Bay's chest.

Lonny looked at his dog, his eyebrows raised. "What's eating you, flea hound?" Then, quickly, he placed the rifle back on the pegs and hung the cow horn beside it.

"Did you think I was goin' somewhere?" Lonny asked.

Bay's grumble burst into a tremendous *bar-roof!* Pa's eyes sharpened and his mouth spread to a smile.

"Did you think I was taking a no-good dog like you hunting?" Lonny asked. Bay's voice came again and the dishes in the cupboard rattled with his bark.

"Don't do old Bay like that, Lonny," Pa said.

3

His tone was rough, but he made no move to stop this game Lonny and Bay always played before going out for a day of hunting.

Lonny cuffed the dog's head and took down the cow horn and gun again. "We'll be back afore night," Lonny said.

"Oh, will you?" Aunt Louise said, sharply. "It better be way afore night unless you like chopping wood in the dark!"

Pa's booming laughter filled the kitchen as boy and dog bounded across the back porch and jumped to the ground. The sun etched shadow patterns on the red clay yard as it filtered through loblolly pines and pecan trees. Beyond was the chicken run and a cornfield still in the shade of Cypress Swamp.

Lonny walked to the split-rail fence and climbed it, then paused, listening. The clink of trace chains and the snort of a mule carried crystal clear in the breathless morning air. He stepped down from the fence and waited, watching a clearing that anyone on the road had to pass before approaching the house.

"Hey, Pa!" Lonny yelled. "Here comes Doc Manners!"

Pa's shoulders almost touched both sides of the door when he came out. Doc Manners waved from down the road and they waved back. Doc always had the latest news about the townfolks and a few good jokes besides. One of the best woodsmen in the county, too. Doc was the only man alive who had wrestled Weakfoot with his bare hands. Once a year, at least, Doc got his hounds and spent a week or two trying to track down the big cat. Because of Weakfoot, Doc carried a leg that grew stiff when the weather changed. The first battle with Weakfoot had been an accident. The hounds got on the cat's scent and Doc unintentionally cornered Weakfoot. The panther sprang on him and only Doc's hounds saved him. He got in one good shot, but the elusive cat was up and gone before he could reload his firearm.

Lonny often thought about Doc's description of the fight and imagined himself holding the big cat at bay. The mule pulled Doc's wagon into the yard and Doc yanked up the reins and shouted insults at the mule for no apparent reason. He sat on the plank seat of the wagon, his feet on either side of the mule's rump, glaring down at Pa and Lonny.

"Howdy, Doc," Pa said, frowning at the abusive language. Pa never raised his voice and no man claimed he had ever heard otherwise.

"Howdy, howdy," Doc said. He leaned far to one side and spit a nugget of tobacco juice to the ground.

"Come in for a cup of coffee?" Pa asked. Only then did Doc step down from the wagon. He stood not quite as tall as Pa. Doc had eyes black as two lumps of coal that could make a good man tremble when Doc lost his temper. Doc's lower lip sank in as if he might have false teeth and never wore the bottom ones.

"Howdy, Spitfire!" Doc said to Lonny. He jabbed a thumb at the boy's ribs, but Lonny, expecting it, jumped aside. Lonny followed the two men inside the house. Aunt Louise was bustling to make the room presentable and Doc caught her with her hair straggling in wisps around her flushed face. She got two mugs for the men as Doc and Pa sat across from one another, their knees almost touching beneath the table.

"What's the news, Doc?" Pa asked.

"Maw Baker's girl, Darlene, got married," Doc said, watching Aunt Louise pour steaming coffee. "Baker's Gin is opening two weeks earlier than usual this year 'cause it's been so infernal dry," he continued. "And I got a tidbit for your hunting warrior," Doc said, jerking his head toward Lonny. He took a loud sip of his coffee before saying more.

"Old Weakfoot," Doc said.

Lonny's fingers tightened on the rifle. Doc was in no hurry to finish, stretching the boy's suspense long as agony.

"What about him?" Pa asked, speaking of Weakfoot.

Doc took yet another sip of his coffee. "Well, I seen him, that's what!"

"Did he kill anything?" Pa asked.

"Not yet," Doc said shortly. His bushy eyebrows lowered. "If I'd had my gun I could have shot him sure as I sit here," Doc said bitterly. "The one day I leave my rifle home and Weakfoot crosses the road so close I thought that lop-eared mule was goin' to climb in the wagon with me!"

Pa's lips drew tight and he stared down at his cup. Lonny remembered stories about the panther, "big as a year-old heifer and black as night." The name Weakfoot came from the soft print the cat's hind foot made. The mighty panther had limped ever since Doc had shot him.

"I'm not wanting to see him myself," Pa said.

Fearing his story was lagging, Doc continued, "He slunk across the road so low his belly was touching the ground. His tail straight out behind him, curving graceful in the middle. He didn't look left and he didn't look right. Just came out one side and disappeared on the other. Gone! Just like a shadow."

"Which way?" Lonny questioned. Pa's eyes cut sharply.

"Never mind which way," Pa said. "Don't

go gitting any ideas about sicking that hound on Weakfoot."

"Went toward Cramer Island," Doc said, as though he hadn't heard Pa. "Come across that road with his ears back, paying no mind to me or that no-count mule!"

Lonny moved to the end of the table. Doc Manners turned to the boy. "He's a killer cat, that one. Mean, and fast as greased lightning, boy! Most cats weigh twenty-five to seventy pounds. I figure Weakfoot tops ninety."

Pa's frown deepened. "Weakfoot is no more dangerous than any other animal, unless he's cornered."

Doc's eyes sparked. For an instant, Lonny thought Doc was angry. Then, shaking his head, Doc said, "Your pa is so peaceable he takes up for killer cats, boy." He softened the bite in his words with a grin that slid sideways on his face.

Pa gazed steadily at Doc. "You know I'm speaking the truth, though."

Doc Manners took another slurp of his coffee. "Maybe I do," he said.

Pa's voice did not change as he spoke again. "Plenty of pigs and calves were lost because that cat got away wounded and too stiff to catch his natural food."

"Through no fault of mine," Doc said tersely. "We hunted Weakfoot for five days and nights, but no dog could catch him and no man moved without a dog to guide him." Doc's eyes narrowed. "With the two hundred dollars bounty that's been put on him over the past five years, you'd think somebody would have hunted that cat down by now. I guess folks still count their blessings and hounds in more ways than dollars."

Pa glanced at Lonny, listening eagerly. "Is Baker's Gin goin' to open exactly two weeks earlier than usual?" Pa asked, changing the subject.

The talk turned to cotton and watermelon and the price of store goods. Soon Doc was pounding one fist on the table and telling Pa how outrageously high prices were. That only rich farmers like Judge White were going to make any money this year. Lonny hitched up his britches to ease the weight of the cow horn on his belt and the cartridges on both pockets. He walked out the door and hopped off the porch. Bay was waiting by the steps.

"Git your nose out of the dirt, Bay." Lonny affectionately slapped the red hound on the rump. "Let's go see what there is left to see this late in the morning."

He climbed the split-rail fence and dropped to the far side. He looked back as Aunt Louise called, "Lonny!"

She ran down the back steps and across the yard in little, short, lady steps. "Lonny"—her face was grave—"you stay away from Cramer Island. You hear?"

Lonny's eyes fell. "Yes'm," he said, quietly. He turned to walk down between rows of corn and Aunt Louise spoke again. "If you got panther-bit, I'd have to chop wood myself."

He turned and looked at her. Her lips trembled a second, then twisted into a small smile, an expression that made him think of his mother, what little he could remember. He smiled in spite of his effort not to.

"If I ever meet old Weakfoot," Lonny said, "it won't be me that gits bit. I'd think about all the things that two hundred dollars bounty would buy—and aim careful."

The smile vanished from Aunt Louise's face and Lonny wished he had left off the bragging.

He studied the worry lines around her eyes and walked back to the fence.

"I won't go near Cramer Island. I promise."

She nodded, satisfied. Holding her apron in one hand, she returned to the house. Bay lay to one side, his long ears in the dirt. Lonny looked at the dog and laughed. "I been fooling around too long for it to be fun anymore, haven't I?" he said. He raised the cow horn to his lips and blew long and hard, then stood listening to the sound echo again and again, rippling away to silence. Bay jumped sideways, bumping the cornstalks in his excitement.

"Well, don't just walk around stiff-legged," Lonny commanded. "Git goin'!"

Bay's voice rose in quick, sharp bursts and Lonny broke into a run. The cornstalks whizzed by as Lonny ran and jumped, twisting his body to avoid fallen stalks. Bay chose the next row over and raced slightly ahead. The buzz of a bee passed Lonny's ear as he ran out of the field of corn into Cypress Swamp.

Wish I could meet up with Weakfoot, Lonny thought. He could imagine the surprise of Doc Manners and Pa and Aunt Louise if he came home dragging the corpse of the panther behind him. Lonny halted and threw up his rifle, just as he would if he suddenly saw Weakfoot.

Pow! He could almost feel the jolt from the weapon as it would feel if he really fired it. *Pow!* Right behind Weakfoot's shoulder he would put the bullet.

Bay waited for the boy, the dog anxiously wagging his tail, whining with excitement.

"All right," Lonny said to the hound. "Might as well quit dreaming. Weakfoot wouldn't be within ten miles of here now."

Abruptly Lonny halted, listening.

He laughed at himself. "Gitting bad off when my mind makes my ears hear something like *that!*" he said aloud. Bay stood stock-still, ears forward, sniffing the air, Lonny's hand on the dog's back.

"Sounded like—" Lonny listened. "Sounded like a panther cry."

The boy cuffed Bay playfully. "Git goin', dog. Me acting like a fool! Goin' to give us both the spooks. Let's hunt coons and possum afore we're both shaking in our tracks."

The dog seemed not to hear Lonny for a moment, still poised, sniffing, listening. Lonny found himself motionless, keenly alert to movement, noises. A gentle breeze murmured in the trees, moss waving lace fingers as the air passed.

"What's the matter with us?" Lonny scoffed. "Come on, Bay, let's go!"

They ran again, the dog leading the way as they raced deeper and deeper into Cypress Swamp.

2

Spanish moss hung like a thousand vegetable spider webs, draping the trees in somber, moody shades of gray. Lonny walked now, picking his way through briar thickets and around chigger-infested cypress knobs poking rounded knees from the moist earth. The odor of stagnant water rose in his nose. Usually this was a pond bed. Water trapped here after the river rose overflowed into this pocket of land. Now, after a long dry spell, only mushy earth remained. It was the reek of dead fish that attracted possums and sometimes coons to this spot. Lonny watched Bay move around the pond bed, the hound's nostrils searching out the scents that tell a dog a thousand tales of what passed this way and how long ago.

"Git on it, Bay," Lonny said, softly, encouraging the animal. Bay's tail wagged with each stride as the dog sniffed, sniffed, then went back and sniffed again. A grumble sounded in Bay's chest and he paused beside a tree a moment, then put his nose to the ground again.

"You fool dog," Lonny said affectionately. "Git on it, Bay."

With another grumble, Bay's head jerked up, then down, and he trotted faster, veering left,

11

right, then back over the same ground again. Bay's chest squeezed out another guttural rumble and the hound's sniffing came louder, more excited.

"Git on it, Bay," Lonny repeated, his voice the same quiet tone. A low bark told Lonny a scent was discovered and the chase was soon to come. Probably a possum this late in the day, Lonny thought. The dry weather made it hard to hold a scent for long and Bay seemed to be taking this one strong. Suddenly, ahead, Bay's voice rose in a musical cry, like a tolling bell, and Lonny's breath came in short gasps as he ran to keep up with the dog.

Bay's yelp rose to a crescendo, reaching full cry as he chased an animal which somewhere ahead was running for its life.

"Hot dig!" Lonny said aloud. He ran faster, dodging cypress knees, unmindful of the threat of snakes, but stepping high and fast. He reached firm ground and ran faster. Out of sight now, Bay insistently called him on. Possum, Lonny thought. But as Bay ran on and on, his thoughts changed. Coon, just as sure as I'm Lonny Bascombe, he decided. Got us a coon! A new excitement urged him forth despite the ache growing in his sides from running so hard.

At last, Bay's voice grew to fever pitch. "About time," Lonny said, as though Bay could hear. "You took your own sweet time doing it, but you got him treed now!"

The boy skirted overhanging limbs and leaped low palmetto clumps. He hit high ground, a glen of flowing sawgrass dulled brown at the tips from lack of rain. Across the clearing, he saw Bay standing with his front feet up a slender sapling.

"A possum after all," Lonny snorted. He

slowed to a walk. No coon would take to a tree so small as the sapling. He looked up and the possum "grinned" down at him, its teeth showing beneath a sharp snout. The critter's beady eyes glared belligerently. Lonny raised his rifle to shoot, then lowered it. He put one foot against the tree and shook it. The possum hugged a branch. Bay jumped against Lonny, his hind feet clawing the boy's leg.

"Git away, dog!" Lonny said, sharply. "Hush your big mouth and wait a minute." Bay barked all the harder as Lonny laid aside his rifle and grabbed the tree in both hands. He shook the sapling violently.

Abruptly, the possum released its hold and fell. It landed on the back of Lonny's neck and immediately Bay jumped up, knocking Lonny to the ground.

"Wait a minute, dog!" Lonny shouted. "Now wait a minute!"

Bay's feet stepped in Lonny's face as dog and possum tangled over his shoulder. Lonny thrashed his arms, shouting, "Back off me, you fool dog! Bay! Git your feet outa my mouth! Here, Bay, look out!"

Lonny grabbed the dog's collar and shoved him out to arm's length. The possum fell to the ground and Lonny rolled away. When he came up, Bay stood over the animal, the dog's tongue hanging from one side of his mouth, his sides heaving from the exertion. The possum was absolutely still. To Bay, the possum was "dead," but Lonny knew better. It was an act nature had taught the possums to help them survive such attacks. If he and Bay should turn their backs, the possum would steal away.

"I hope you satisfied yourself," Lonny said, but his voice was not harsh. "Letting a possum run you over all the county, I thought sure it was a coon. That was bad enough, but you treeing him on me doesn't make me laugh a lot."

Lonny climbed to his feet and picked his trousers clean of beggar's-lice. He looked around the glen and realized he'd never been here before. He listened to the cry of mockers and butcher-birds screaming insults at one another. He slung the possum in a sack, over one shoulder. Bay immediately lost interest and his nose dropped to the ground seeking new scents.

"Next time pick a critter with shorter legs and less energy," Lonny said. He watched the hound make a wide circle, then go off into the woods. Lonny walked, unhurried, following.

Bay seemed to have the scent of the possum still in his nostrils and he was not hunting with as much interest anymore. Lonny pushed through heavy underbrush and blackberry brambles.

"Can't you go any way but the thickest?" he sputtered, as an unseen web caught him fully in the face. He stumbled on through the matted growth and stopped, raking his mouth to clean away the web. He wiped his lips on the back of one sleeve and looked around for Bay. Lonny gave a low whistle and the hound came to his side.

"Let's git out of here," Lonny said. He realized he was whispering. He glanced around and around and his heart almost stood still.

"Cramer Island!"

Of course, he hadn't recognized it because he never approached it from this direction. He had always taken the flat-bottomed boat and come up the river. Lonny dropped the wriggling possum to the ground. A vague uneasiness gripped him. Pa would understand how he had chased a possum here without realizing it, but Aunt Louise never would. "I won't go near Cramer Island. I promise." That was what he had said. Lonny turned completely around, looking for the path that would lead him out. The underbrush had closed behind him. Which was the shortest way home?

Lonny pushed his way back through the blackberry bramble. He stumbled across a creek, soaking his boots. Had he crossed that creek coming in here? Bay sensed his master's growing anxiety and stayed close beside Lonny. The glen! Almost straight ahead. Lonny broke into a run.

Suddenly, Bay halted so fast his hind legs passed the front ones and he nearly sat down. The hound's hair bristled along the spine, Bay standing very still. Lonny stepped to Bay's side. A low moan in the distance began with a whisper and rose, higher, lounder, to a piercing scream and stopped abruptly!

Goosebumps prickled Lonny's flesh and blood drummed in his ears as he held his breath. He grabbed Bay's collar and the dog whimpered. No longer were the mockers and butcher-birds quarreling. Even the wind in the treetops had hushed, the swamp waiting, waiting. A shiver passed through Bay's body and the dog strained forward.

"How come it's so unnatural quiet?" Lonny whispered.

He touched the cow horn on his belt. Maybe he ought to blow it one time and scare something to sound. Still holding Bay's collar tightly, Lonny crawled forward beneath thick vines. For a reason he could not name, he made as little noise as possible. He stopped at the edge of the glen and crouched beside his dog, muzzling Bay's mouth with one hand. Bay leaned against him, trembling, his nose flaring, smelling, listening.

This wasn't the same glen!

Where was the sapling in which the possum had been treed? Why was the sawgrass green even to the tips, not dry the way he remembered the other glen? "We went the wrong way," Lonny groaned. They were now deeper into Cramer Island. His hands were perspiring so much, the stock of the rifle was slippery in his grip.

Again, nearer than before, the low moaning cry started as a sigh and rose, higher, louder, piercing the air, and stopped! It came to a halt as though it had been chopped off at its very height, leaving the silence that followed even heavier than before. Every living thing must surely be rigid, alert, trembling as Lonny and Bay now trembled, waiting, listening.

Bay leaped forward and Lonny grabbed him and clamped down on Bay's mouth to trap the *bar-roof!* that almost escaped.

"Be still!" Lonny hissed. "Hush!"

Once more, like a far wind building, the cry began in a low hushed tone, rising to an ear-splitting shriek. Then, as it became unbearable, the sound abruptly stopped!

Cold fingers of sweat traced Lonny's back and ran down under his arms. He had an overwhelming urge to leap up and run, as fast and as hard as he could, run for home. Yet he did not even move the muscles it took to brush away the black gnats swarming around his face. With his free hand, Lonny triggered the safety on his rifle and thumbed back the hammer. The click sounded unnaturally loud in the deathly quiet after the last cry. Bay was no longer whimpering, but the dog bucked once, twisting to free himself.

"Hold still, Bay," Lonny demanded.

Might be smart to turn Bay loose and let him ferret out the strange animal with such a chilling cry. Lonny held the dog even closer. The boy's eyes moved slowly around the perimeter of the glen, watching for any movement to help him locate the creature.

When it came again, the scream was now so near that Lonny jumped and Bay slipped from his grasp. The dog bolted to one side, along the edge of the woods, then into a dense growth of vines.

"Bay! Come back here! Bay!"

Even as the moaning cry rose in volume, Bay's full-throated hunting voice joined it and the two sounds merged in discord. Lonny stumbled forward into the glen of knee-high sawgrass. He heard Bay's voice turn from the cry of the hunter to a howling scream as dog and adversary clashed head-on. Lonny ran forward to the hole where the dog had disappeared.

"Bay!" He tried to push through the matted tangle. "Bay! Come here!"

The snarling, spitting growls told of the fight taking place in the underbrush. The crash of the bodies and the frenzied sounds of anger painted a vivid picture in Lonny's mind of what must be happening. His rifle snagged on a scuppernong vine and fell to the ground. Lonny snatched it up, throwing his body against the woven wall of vegetation. The limbs of stunted water oaks, muscadine vines, and ivy made him bend almost double to pass beneath them.

Lonny heard Bay howl in pain. For a breathtaking instant there was dead silence. Then hound and prey clashed again, farther away from Lonny. The vines connecting each tree to another relayed the shock of the animals' bodies rolling, snarling, spitting.

Lonny fell to his knees to see beneath the dense foliage.

"Bay!"

Lonny crawled into the cavelike area beneath the vegetation. He was getting his rifle dirty and his clothes wet, and he didn't care. He had to save his dog. Lonny tore his way into the clearing, kicking himself free of the last clinging vine, scrambling to get up. With a strength he did not know he possessed, he snatched his leg and heard the trouser rip and give. He wheeled, crouching, a gasp escaping from his throat. The wicked eyes of a black face came toward him in long, bounding leaps.

"Weakfoot!"

3

Doc Manners had said, "Weakfoot is big, and black, and vicious! A killer cat. With the speed of greased lightning."

Lonny dived to the ground and rolled to one side, pointing the rifle automatically. The deafening roar of the shot made his ears hum. The panther jumped, twisted crazily, and fell. At once, it was on its feet again and Lonny's tongue went dry.

Weakfoot's glistening coat of blue-black hair was stained crimson. For a moment, boy and beast looked at one another.

Bay crashed into the glen going straight for the cat. Weakfoot jumped by reflex action and the dog missed his charge. The panther reared back on it haunches, fangs bared, ears flat, hissing. Lonny fumbled to reload the rifle and dropped the cartridge. He pulled another from his pocket but his hand trembled so, he could scarcely hold it. The hound wheeled and now faced Weakfoot, hair bristling, growling. The panther was momentarily stunned by the grazing bullet. Weakfoot did not attack, nor try to escape. Bay darted forward, head low, and the cat's raking claws were a swish! Bay howled and rolled under the

19

cats' powerful paw. Three stripes of red showed
in the dog's side.

"Hee-yow!" Lonny yelled. He raised the cow
horn and blew long and hard, the sound caroming
from earth to sky across the glen, through Cypress
Swamp and over the marshlands. Weakfoot suddenly leaped forward on the hound, its fangs
sinking in Bay's shoulder. With incredible speed,
the cat's rear legs came up under the dog's belly,
clawing. Lonny screamed in frustration as his
fingers fumbled another bullet and dropped it in
the grass.

Weakfoot turned with a single leap, stumbled
in pain as it hit on the wounded shoulder, then
limped off in silent, short strides, the long tail
trailing behind. Lonny fell to his knees beside
the dog.

"Bay! Oh, no, Bay!" The dog's tongue lolled
from the side of his mouth into sandy soil. The
dog panted, but his breathing came shallow, each
breath slightly shorter than the one before.

"Shame!" Lonny cried. "I was a coward!"
He lifted the dog's head to his lap, crying, softly
speaking. "I got you killed, Bay. I got you killed
because I was afraid."

Bay quivered, his panting drawing shorter
and shorter.

"I couldn't help it, Bay. My fingers trembled
I couldn't git a bullet in the rifle. I couldn't help
it. I'm sorry. Oh, Bay, I'm sorry."

The hound's breathing was quicker, more
shallow. The dog coughed and stretched, a shiver
making the raised legs quiver.

"Oh, Bay, don't die."

Bay's body shuddered and a long sigh left
the dog's lungs. One final tremor seemed to shake
the warmth from the dog's body. Lonny stared
down at the lifeless animal. He rocked slowly

back and forth. "Oh, no," he whispered. "That cat's killed my dog. I let that cat kill Bay." Tears fell on Bay's shoulder. "I'm sorry, Bay. I was a coward. I'm sorry."

Suddenly, he shouted in the direction Weakfoot had gone. "I'll git you, Weakfoot! I'm goin' to hang your sorry hide on my barn door. You hear me, cat? I'll git you!"

He held the dog's head in his lap, sobbing, cursing himself for cowardice, ignoring the setting sun and the coming of darkness.

Weakfoot limped slowly toward the den, below and behind the sheltering limbs of a giant oak which grew against the clay bank. The cave meant safety. It nestled halfway up the bank with the opening hidden by overhanging grass and the foliage of the oak. The cat leaped for a low limb but fell askew with pain streaking through one shoulder. Panting, the panther gathered strength. Then with a mightly effort, the cat bounded two jumps and sprang to the lowest crotch of the oak. The terrible pain brought no cry, not a whimper. Each step sent agonizing fire into the crippled leg when weight fell on it. Favoring the hurt leg, cautiously, the cat walked out on a limb, then into the den. This pain! This searing sudden hurt that followed a loud noise was made by man and it left the legs stiff, no longer agile enough to catch game for food. The fleet escape of a rabbit would leave the cat longing and hungry with such a weak leg.

Three mottled kittens, brown with darker spots, met Weakfoot within the den. Weakfoot licked the cubs, cleansing each, reassuring them, even before she licked her own shoulder as high as she could reach. She collapsed on one side, breathing hard, her tail moving only at the tip.

The kittens tumbled over one another to reach the mother, seeking nourishment. Instinct told her the babies must have milk. To have milk, she must have food. Painfully, she adjusted her position to ease the burning of her wound. The happy sounds of the feeding kittens gave her no comfort this time. She let her head lie on the floor of the den, eyes closed. Soon, when the pain was less, she must seek food in the area where man lived. She never went there anymore. She had, for a while, once before in her life. Now, Weakfoot was frightened.

Night cloaked the cornfield behind the house when Lonny reached the edge of Cypress Swamp. Crickets filled the air with their dry-cry of tiny staccato chirps, like a thousand miniature combs being thumbed by a thousand miniature men. He walked up the same row of corn he and Bay had run down this morning. He fought the ache in his chest. *That fool dog*, he thought. He choked back new tears. *Wonderful fool dog*.

Aunt Louise had said, "You better be home afore night, unless you like chopping wood in the dark!"

Now, under the shadow of evening, Lonny was thankful he would not be seen returning alone. He dreaded facing Pa and Aunt Louise. He climbed the split-rail fence, dropped to the other side, and leaned his rifle there. The axe was inside the barn door.

Lonny brought the axe down on a length of tree and heard it whack! "There, Weakfoot!" he said aloud, and pulled the axe free. Whack! "Take that in your head!" He worked the axe handle up and down to free the blade from the chopping stump. He froze as a footstep sounded behind him.

"Lonny?" Pa's deep voice.

"Yes sir?"

"I already chopped kindling, boy. Come eat supper."

Lonny swallowed a lump rising in his throat and put away the axe. Pa was waiting for him. Together, they walked toward the back porch.

"Catch anything today?" Pa questioned.

Pa would be very angry when he learned Weakfoot was wounded again. The panther would be raiding farms for pigs and calves, And Aunt Louise had forbidden Lonny to go near Cramer Island. So before he could stop himself, Lonny heard his own voice saying, "One old possum."

Pa grunted and one large hand touched the boy's shoulder. "Aunt Louise cooked biscuits," Pa said. "So, just this once, I chopped wood so you could eat them while they're hot." Lonny followed Pa through the back door. Aunt Louise turned from the wood stove, a pan of hot biscuits held with her apron.

"Wash your face and—" Aunt Louise looked at Lonny, her eyes wide.

Pa saw her expression and turned. Lonny's shirt had gotten ripped and torn when Bay was trying to get the possum that fell on Lonny's shoulders. The blood of the dog was on him, too. His arms were caked with it, his shirt soaked in it.

"Did you git hurt?" Pa asked, his voice quiet.

"No sir. Bay—Bay slung possum blood on me."

A lie! He told Pa a lie. The fact that he had must surely show on his face. Lonny turned his head and walked quickly toward the bedroom.

"Lonny," Pa asked, "where's your dog?"

Lonny answered from the door. "He's out in the swamps. The fool dog—he run—" Lonny

24

couldn't finish. Tears rose in his eyes and his voice choked.

"He'll be back, boy. He's been lost a dozen times, and he always finds his way back."

Lonny shut his bedroom door behind him. He could not believe he had lied to Pa and Aunt Louise. His shame for his fear of the cat was now joined by his shame for the lie. Lonny fell headlong across the bed and pushed his face into the covers. Muffling his voice, he cried.

Three days later, rain came at last to break the long dry spell. Big, moist drops fell groundward from thick clouds overhead. A week passed and it was still falling, very slowly, but steadily, pausing now and then to let the trees drip themselves before coming again in a drizzle.

"Well, sir," Doc Manners said, sitting down at the table with Pa, "the rain is good luck, I reckon." Pa agreed.

"Maybe we'll git a late crop or two yet," Doc added. Aunt Louise poured coffee for Pa and Doc.

"What's the news, Doc?" Pa asked.

Doc's black eyes fixed on Pa. "Weakfoot is the news," Doc said.

"I don't want any more talk about that cat," Pa said quickly. "If we leave him alone, he won't bother us, and I got no notion of bothering him."

"Trouble is," Doc argued, "Weakfoot ain't leaving us alone."

Pa's hand balled into a fist. "What do you mean?"

"Leb Daniels lost a shoat last week," Doc said. He took a noisy sip of his coffee. Aunt Louise frowned. She didn't like people "calling" their coffee that way.

"Might have got lost," Pa said, referring to

the pig. Lonny's heart beat faster as Doc continued to explain.

"Might have, " Doc agreed. "But Sam White lost hisself a newborn calf three nights later. Then another pig walked off and got lost from Ralph Breese's place." Doc sipped his coffee again. "Seems funny something gits lost about once every three to five days, don't it?"

Pa's fist suddenly struck the table and the coffee mugs did a short dance. "Why should that cat all of a sudden start raiding again? Almost three years and not a pig or calf stolen!"

"Weakfoot's just a killer cat, that's all," Doc said calmly.

Pa snorted in disgust and turned sideways in his chair. His eyes darted here and there as they always did when he was angry. Then his eyes stopped, and he stared at Lonny.

Lonny wiped one sweating hand down his pants leg under Pa's steady, piercing glare. Doc Manners followed Pa's gaze and he too looked at the boy. Lonny felt the blood drain from his face.

Pa leaned forward, resting one elbow on a corner of the table. "Lonny," Pa said, his voice ominous, "where is your dog?"

Aunt Louise stood unmoving, her back to them. Doc looked down in his coffee mug, knowing something was wrong between Pa and the boy. In the ten days since the dog and panther fought, there had been no mention of Bay. Pa just assumed the dog would find his way home after becoming lost in the swamp. Lonny saw Pa's face coloring with anger.

"Answer me, boy," Pa ordered.

"Dead," Lonny cried. "Bay's dead, Pa!"

4

Stunned, Pa and Doc and Aunt Louise stared at Lonny.

Pa's voice was softer now. "Did you accidentally shoot Bay, Lonny?"

Lonny shook his head, fighting to subdue tears that threatened to come.

"What happened, boy?"

Quietly, with shame, Lonny told them how Bay had attacked the panther and the cat had killed him. But he could not force himself to tell of his fumbling fingers and the fear that paralyzed him. He could tell Pa perhaps, another time. Doc Manners would never understand such a fear. Hadn't Doc wrestled Weakfoot with his bare hands?

"Where did it happen?" Pa asked.

Lonny swallowed, his mouth bitter. "Cramer Island."

Aunt Louise gasped. "Oh, Lonny," she said, "you promised not to go there."

"I didn't mean to," Lonny cried. "I was following Bay and he was running a possum. I never went to Cramer Island in that direction afore and I didn't know we'd gone so far. I didn't mean to, Aunt Louise! That's why I—why I didn't tell the truth."

"Which way did the cat run for, Spitfire?" Doc asked.

"South."

"You had no cause to lie to me, boy," Pa said.

Lonny's chin dropped to his chest, his head down. "Yes sir," he replied.

"We should've been out hunting that cat the next day," Pa said. "Now we got a wounded panther on our hands and a dangerous one at that. Weakfoot's goin' to have a craving for easy prey and be short-tempered about getting it."

"He already was," Doc injected.

Pa turned back to Doc and the subject changed. But Lonny could see veins standing out on Pa's neck and Pa's face was flushed. Disappointed, Lonny thought bitterly. Pa is disappointed in me. The boy left the house and walked to the barn, his feet leaving prints in the muddy yard. After a while, Doc Manners came out and took his leave. Pa stood on the back porch after Doc's wagon disappeared beyond the clearing.

"Lonny!"

Lonny wanted to run—deep into Cypress Swamp. Every muscle ached to flee, but he walked out of the barn and stood where Pa could see him. Pa stood absolutely motionless for what seemed an eternity. He came down the steps and across the yard.

"Come sit in the barn with me, Son," Pa suggested. They sat on a bench where harness was sometimes kept. Lonny could not keep his eyes on Pa's face.

"Don't ever tell me something that isn't truth," Pa said at last. His face was frowned up, like he was hurting deep inside.

"I'm sorry, Pa," Lonny said. "I did it so quick! I'm so ashamed."

"Being honest is about all that gives a man

pride," Pa said. "When a man ain't honest, other men sense it and he loses the most precious thing he owns—the high respect of his friends. Now, boy, let's forget it. The lie don't count unless it were to happen again, which it won't."

Lonny knew, to be completely free of his tormented conscience, he had to tell Pa about the fight with the cat and his fear that had cost Bay his life. He opened his mouth to speak, but Pa arose quickly and walked out of the barn.

I'm goin' to git that cat, Lonny thought. Remembering the sleek body, the lightning movements, and the hissing beast, Lonny's blood seemed to chill. He forced himself to think, I'm going to git that cat! I got it to do.

Deep inside, rising like a mighty winged bird from a still pond, beating up and up and up, the thought wavered. The vivid memory of the fangs and claws of Weakfoot flashed across his mind. *Can you do it? Can you do it, coward? Can you?*

Three days later found Lonny sitting in the buckboard seat of their wagon, cotton piled high in the crib behind him. Wagons one behind the other lined the road to Baker's Gin and stretched out around the bend a quarter of a mile, waiting their turn. Off to the side, beneath pecan and willow trees, men and boys sat in small groups, not too far from their wagons so they could pull up and take the next place forward when a wagon finished.

The story of Lonny's encounter with Weakfoot was the subject of conversation everywhere. Men spoke of how Lonny had come face to face with the panther. Doc Manners must have spread the word from highland to low. The story in its telling grew of itself until Lonny was said to have grappled with the deadly cat with his bare hands, just as Doc was reputed to have done. They told of Lonny's coming home covered "with the panther's blood."

Down the line, a shrill whistle blasted the air and everybody climbed to their feet and went to pull up their wagons a few yards. Another wagon went under the hot tin roof of the gin to be unloaded.

Bucky Landers climbed in the wagon with Lonny. Bucky had two teeth missing which had been knocked out when he rode a running horse under a low limb in the woods. Common sense told a man not to run a horse in the woods. One thing Bucky lacked was common sense.

"My redbone hound had her puppiess," Bucky whistled. His missing teeth made him whistle any word with an *s* in it.

"Goin' to make the finesst hunting dogss you ever ssaw," Bucky continued. His voice lowered and he cut his eyes at Lonny.

"I heard about old Bay gitting kilt. Thought maybe," he shrugged his shoulders. "Thought maybe you'd like one of my pupss."

Lonny's eyes narrowed suspiciously. Bucky Landers had never paid him any mind. Before he could accept or refuse, Bucky's eyes sparked.

"Next time you goin' to hunt that cat, Lonny, how about letting me go along? I'll bring my dogss and—"

"I ain't hunting down that cat!" Lonny snapped.

Bucky could not believe his ears.

"I wasn't hunting him afore and I ain't hunting him now," Lonny said sharply.

Bucky Landers stared at Lonny, his face blank. Slowly, his lips spread. The hole where his missing teeth had been made his face look lopsided. "I reckon you got a belly full, after all," he said. Bucky hopped down from the wagon and looked up at Lonny. A short laugh escaped Bucky's throat and he poked his tongue through the hole in his teeth and licked his lips in quick, short movements like a snake.

"I reckon maybe I'd be sscared too, if Weakfoot jumped me like he did you."

Lonny's face flushed and his cheeks burned. He glared at the mule's back. Bucky laughed again.

"I don't guess it takess but one meet with Weakfoot to make ssome men yeller. Lookss to me like the hound done most of the fighting—ain't that sso?"

In an instant, Lonny leaped from the wagon. Bucky wheeled and Lonny fell to the ground, stumbling to one knee. He was up in a second and his anger drove him toward Bucky's leering face. Bucky ducked and sidestepped. Lonny hit the side of his wagon. The men from the gin came and formed a ring around the two boys. Lonny lunged again and Bucky's foot caught his ankle. The ground came up and with a sickening thud, Lonny sprawled face forward. Standing over him, Bucky laughed.

"Lonny wass jusst sshowing me how old Weakfoot come at him!"

A ripple of laughter rose from the crowd. Lonny sucked air into his lungs and crawled to his feet.

"Sshow uss ssome more, Lonny," Bucky said, making his tone that of a child begging candy.

"Come on, Bascombe," somebody added, "give us a sample of what happened. Did you grab Weakfoot by the neck, or the tail?"

Their laughter throbbed in Lonny's ears. He

brushed dirt off his trousers and walked back to the wagon with his head down.

"Scared," he heard Bucky say. "Plain scared."

I'm a fool, Lonny thought. A clumsy fool.

Bucky had whipped him without raising a hand. That hurt worse than a broken leg. If Bucky had struck him with something, a stick or rock! But Bucky had not even hit him with his fist.

"Don't pay them any mind."

The girl stood close to the wagon on the far side from where Lonny and Bucky had scuffled. She stood in the shade of the cotton piled high behind Lonny.

"Bucky's a blowhard," she said. Lonny squinted his eyes and studied her face. Shirley Landers was Bucky's half-sister. She wasn't really a Landers at all, but when Shirley's father died Ma Landers had gone back to using the name she'd had longest. Now they were all Landerses—they lived about a quarter of a mile from Lonny's house.

"I reckon you want to talk about Weakfoot, too," Lonny said.

"No."

He wiped grit from his chin with the back of one sleeve. She watched, saying nothing.

"I just ate dirt from your brother," Lonny said.

"You were mad. Might be different if you hadn't of been."

Lonny chewed his tongue a moment, looking at her.

"Were you afraid?" Shirley asked. Lonny knew she was speaking of Weakfoot.

He nodded. He half expected her to run away and tell everyone he had admitted his fear to her. She shielded her eyes from the sun with one hand. "I'd of been afraid," she confessed. "I'd of been so afraid I would have died. I don't figure there's any shame to it, either."

"Maybe not for a girl," Lonny allowed.

Shirley Landers stepped forward, reassured. "Lonny, did you hurt Weakfoot? I mean, hurt him bad?"

"In the shoulder. It was a glancing shot. Not enough to stop him, though."

Her voice dropped low. "My uncle—Tom Smutt—he ran away into the swamp after he—" Lonny knew the story of Tom Smutt.

"Smutt killed his own brother," Shirley said and her eyes widened with the words. "Some folks say Weakfoot ate Smutt and possums scattered his bones."

Lonny did not know how to react. Smutt was Shirley's uncle. It was Ma Landers' brother Smutt had killed.

"It might be Smutt and Weakfoot is the same, now."

"The same?" Lonny questioned. "How do you mean?"

"You believe what you eat becomes a part of you, don't you?" Shirley asked. "Liver makes blood, collards give you strength, cornbread and peas stick to your ribs—hog brains and scrambled eggs makes the brain healthy. You believe that?"

Lonny nodded, dumbfounded.

"Then," Shirley whispered, "killing Weakfoot would be kin to—to killing a man. I mean, if Weakfoot ate Smutt. Wouldn't it?"

Lonny stirred uneasily before her intense gaze, her eyes narrowed and filled with a strange fire. She pressed nearer.

"Maybe so," Lonny agreed. "But Smutt was a killer. More the reason to kill Weakfoot."

Shirley's eyes softened and her thin lips relaxed. She stood looking at Lonny an uncomfortably long time. He saw a shimmer of tears in her eyes. He tried to think of something he could say, but no words came to mind. Then the girl turned and ran away, down the road by the waiting wagons.

"Yeller berries on the vine, yeller is the coward's spine," Bucky Landers chanted as he passed Lonny's wagon.

Up at the gin the whistle blew again and the wagons were mounted anew by riders, each one clicking his tongue to awaken the mules dozing where they stood. A rattle of trace chains signaled that the moving file was taking new positions and Lonny flicked the reins, sucking air between pursed lips, urging his own mule, "Move up!"

He moved as though in a trance. His mind was not on the mule, or the ginning of cotton. Not even Bucky's jeering was penetrating Lonny's thoughts.

I got to kill that cat, Lonny declared to himself. I got it to do.

5

The first rays of sunshine had not reached the shutters over Lonny's window and he was awake. Shivering from the morning chill, he put on his clothing. Already the sounds of a new day had started. Pa and Aunt Louise would be up shortly.

The boy took down his cow horn and attached it to his belt. He lifted his rifle off the rack and filled two pockets with cartridges.

"Lonny?" Aunt Louise called from her room.

"Yes ma'am?"

"Be back for lunch, boy."

He stuffed cornbread and a piece of fried pigskin and a handful of cookies into a sack. He went to Aunt Louise's door and raised the sack for her to see.

"I got lunch," he said. Aunt Louise smiled, her eyes puffed with sleep. She nodded. In the other bedroom, Pa turned in his sleep and the bedsprings protested under his weight. Lonny tiptoed out the back door, easing it shut behind him. He had done most of his chores last night after coming home from Baker's Gin. He paused at the barn to throw scratch feed to the chickens, then climbed the split-rail fence and ran through the cornfield.

When I find that cat, Lonny reminded himself, I mostly got to keep a clear head. Stay calm and move cautious.

He walked unhurried, following the route he and Bay had taken the day they ran into Weakfoot. Somewhere, far ahead, a 'gator bellowed, the sound breaking the morning hush. A heron rose in flight as Lonny approached a mirror-smooth pond. The pocket of land had filled with water since the day Bay discovered the scent of the possum here.

Alert for snakes, Lonny pushed through knee-high palmetto fronds, wet muck underfoot sucking his boots. Using the stock of his rifle, he pushed aside a huge spider web, heavy laden with pearls of dew. An orange-and-black dancing spider raced for safety. Lonny paid him no mind. He skirted a blackberry bramble and walked faster as he approached the glen.

Lonny heard the chatter of a fox squirrel and without thinking, raised his rifle to bag the animal. The squirrel hugged a pine bough.

"Go ahead and shoot—spook Weakfoot!" Lonny reprimanded himself angrily. "Shoot! Tell him you was coming ten miles away."

The silhouette of the squirrel disappeared as the animal scampered to the opposite side of the pine.

Lonny's heart quickened as he stooped to go under an overgrowth of vines and low limbs where the fight between Weakfoot and Bay had taken place. Bay's carcass had been carried away by coons, possums, and swamp rats, maybe even by Weakfoot.

Lower and lower the ceiling of growth forced Lonny until he was crawling. The earth was bare of grass. Only the root stock of vegetation grew here, climbing into the matted tangle over him, searching sunlight. Ever mindful of snakes, especially the dreaded black body of the sluggish cottonmouth water moccasin, Lonny continued to crawl. At last, he stood again in bright sunshine.

The boy paused to straighten his back. Jorees flitted in a persimmon tree. The call of a crow to its brothers split the air with a harsh *cawt, cawt, cawt!* Cypress trees, for which the swamp was named, pushed skyward to unbelievable heights. Spanish moss hung in trails ten and twelve feet long. This was the part of the swamp that people claimed would swallow up a man. Lonny used his hunting knife to mark the trees as a guide for himself. He pushed forward, marking trees as he went. Only when he reached another glen did he realize the sun was noon-high or a little after.

No sign of Weakfoot.

He ate his cornbeard and pigskin and wished he had brought something to drink. The cookies he ate as he walked. He waded through water ankle-deep, avoiding cypress boles as big around as a man's arms could reach. Each bole crawled with ticks and chiggers. He took his steps with care, feeling for depth and testing the ground. He was wary, for a deep pocket of water and quicksand was always a threat when wading in swamplands.

A river, wider than any Lonny knew existed in these parts, stopped him. The black waters moved so slowly he could not be sure the river moved at all. He followed the bank a short distance, then turned inland. He decided to head for home when he involuntarily raised his head and sniffed.

Smoke, he thought. Must be I've circled myself and come close to somebody's home.

There was no need to walk through the swamp when he could take a road back to the house. It was obvious he would never find Weakfoot just wandering around. He followed his nose, sniffing now and then for a trace of the elusive odor of burning wood. No, it didn't smell exactly like wood smoke alone. It smelled—

Lonny halted, not really believing what he saw. It was so expertly camouflaged that Lonny didn't realize it until he was on it—a complete campsite. He made a full turn and saw he stood in the center of the encampment. A lean-to had been constructed against a massive oak tree and the builder had used honeysuckle vines to tie the structure together. The roof was overlaid palmetto fronds. Only the eyes of a huntsman looking for it would have seen the shelter. A recent kill hung from the oak. Tepee fashion, evergreens leaned against the kill, funneling smoke on it from hickory chips smoldering below. The hickory and the odor of curing meat was what Lonny had smelled.

In a hole in the sand, the campfire had been banked for the day and atop glowing embers sat an earthen crock. Lonny recognized sassafras roots sticking out of the bowl. Somebody was making sassafras tea. Beneath his feet, the river sand was packed hard from much use. This was no overnight or weekend camp. Somebody used this place daily. Lonny realized he was crouching. He stood erect.

"Hello!" Lonny called.

His voice came back in echoes. "Hello . . . hello. . . ."

"Anybody here?"

"Here . . . here . . . here . . . ," the swamp replied.

The kill hung to cure was swarming with gnats and flies, their wings a constant ugly hum. The hickory chips smoking beneath the kill had not chased away the insects yet.

Just started to cure it when they heard me coming, Lonny guessed! He stepped nearer, examining the kill.

That's a hog! He parted the tent of evergreens. Most likely a shoat.

Why would anyone come way out here to smoke a side of pork? Unless—

The hair on the back of Lonny's neck rose. He became acutely aware of eyes that must be watching him.

Stolen shoat! Lonny realized. Sure as I stand here.

Act calm. Like you looked and realized nothing.

"Hello-o!" he yelled again, louder than before.

"Elloooo . . . loooo . . . oooo. . . ." His echo came rippling back from across the bayous and lakes. With deliberate calm and measured movements, Lonny shrugged his shoulders and turned. He left the buzzing of the insects behind, walking back the way he had come. He entered the cool shade of a tall stand of cypress trees, resisting the urge to break and run.

Yellow eyes watched Lonny depart. The boy would tell! He would return to his people and tell about the stolen pig and the hidden camp and men would come in great numbers, armed with dogs and guns.

Quietly, on feet with soles of callused flesh, the thief slipped down from a tree and landed silently where the boy had stood a moment ago. He bent low until his bare back was no higher than the tips of sawgrass. He ran until he spied the boy, still walking. Maybe he should kill this boy. Quickly, quietly, do it and let everybody think the boy had been 'gator-eaten. Still, the men would come if he did that. Perhaps they would find his camp if they came.

Maybe the boy did not understand what he had seen. If he did, he would talk, wouldn't he? The thief debated—kill him or not?

Keeping low, the pursuer followed, moving quickly and halting after brief runs forward. When he stopped, he stood absolutely still except for his yellow eyes darting, watching, wary. In his frozen attitude, he was but a patch of sunlight, a piece of the swamp. So that, when Lonny turned to be sure he wasn't being followed, he looked right over the man who stood motionless not sixty yards away.

Lonny thought, Just my mind playing shadow tricks on me. He got down on all fours and crawled into the tunnel of thicket through which he must pass to get back to the glen. It was darker under here now that the sun had settled into the late afternoon hours. He pulled himself along the endless tunnel. He paused. Had he heard something? Over there to the right. A sudden flurry of the bushes made him cry out.

"Oh!"

Silence. He waited, heart pounding. Nothing. One minute passed, then two. He did not move.

"Hssssssss-sst!"

The sound made Lonny's lips quiver, and his mouth turned dry. That sound had been burned into his memory. He could still remember the fangs and sleek black coat glistening with blood. Yes, he knew that sound and would not likely ever forget the curled lips and red throat from which it had come. It was the same hissing, spitting noise Weakfoot had made just as the panther had prepared to pounce forward and sink its fangs into Bay and rip out the dog's belly.

"Hyar!" Lonny yelled. "Hyar!"

He threw himself on one side and fired into the thicket toward that awful hissing cry. "Hyar! Hyar!" Panic seized every fiber of his body and he yelled again and again, "Hyar!" He did not take time to reload his rifle. Rather, as the blood-curdling sound rose again, he clawed his way toward the light of the glen, far, far ahead.

The snarl of the beast came again and Lonny wheeled, eyes wide, trembling with terror. He jammed a cartridge into his weapon and fired back down the way he had come.

"Git!" he shrieked. "Git out of here!"

He fumbled another cartridge from his pocket, raking out others that dropped into the mushy ground beside him. He saw his hands tremble as they had trembled the day he had allowed Bay to die under the cat's fangs and claws. He tried to steady them and the effort made them quiver all the more.

Coward, coward, coward!

He pushed the new bullet into the chamber and snapped the breech.

Think calm. Be calm.

"Hss-st—hsss-ssst!"

The scream of the panther was almost behind him and Lonny pitched to one side, bringing up the rifle in the same motion. He heard his own sobs and saw the rifle barrel shaking like a reed in high wind. He would be lucky if he hit Weakfoot even if he had time to aim, which he would not have time to do in this thicket!

A furious rustling in the underbrush drove away Lonny's last thought of fighting. Panic overcame him and he tore through the tunnel, crying aloud, plunging into the glen. He hit firm ground and came to his feet in a dead run as fast as his legs could carry him. Through briar thickets and sawgrass, leaping higher than he had ever leaped, running faster than he had ever run—away from the rising scream of the panther behind him. Until his lungs begged for rest and his sides ached, he ran. His spittle tasted of copper and his breath came in gasps that seared his throat. Behind him, over and over, the cry of the panther rose and fell, echoing into the swamp.

The thief watched the boy go, running in terror. The man's yellow eyes glinted as he smiled. That ought to give the boy something to talk about besides a little stolen pork. The thief cackled to himself, his voice subdued and heard only by himself. Not many boys had ever fought off a panther. The thief laughed, his mirth showing only in his face, not in the sound he made, for he made no sound. He thought, *That is a good joke to play. A good sound of the panther, too! The boy really thought a cat was upon him. Very good sound!*

6

Doc Manners usually came calling on a Thursday. Lonny had been dreading the meeting. He was ashamed that Doc knew or might have guessed the truth about Lonny's encounter with Weakfoot. And by now, Doc would know of the boy's futile clash with Bucky Landers at Baker's Gin.

A steady drizzle fell the entire day, and as afternoon turned toward evening it looked as if Doc wasn't coming. By nightfall, Lonny was chopping wood, thinking about his close scrape yesterday. He had told no one. The camp itself seemed so unimportant he had not given it another thought.

Lonny was carrying kindling toward the house when he heard a horse coming down the road. The speed of the animal's feet upon the ground made Lonny pause. He caught a glimpse of a rider passing a clearing. It was Sherman Prather, the mailman who filled in when Joe Beaudry was sick. The last time Sherman rode up that way, it was to get Pa to come help fight a woods fire behind Beaudry's barn. Sherman reined in and his horse pranced nervously.

"Where's your pa?" Sherman shouted.

Pa came out of the house, his suspenders over bare shoulders, shirtless. Sherman yanked up the reins and his mount turned a complete circle in its own tracks.

"Better come quick!" Sherman yelled. "Doc Manners is dying!"

Pa took a short step forward, staring at the rider. "What happened?" Pa asked.

"Weakfoot!"

The horse skittered and Sherman Prather hugged the saddle with his knees. "Doc and his hounds set out for Cramer Island tracking Weakfoot this morning after Doc found a pig slaughtered," Sherman related. "Doc came dragging back this afternoon. Weakfoot jumped him. He's near about dead. Better hurry!"

Digging his heels into the horse's sides, Sherman leaned forward in the stirrups. Mud flew from the animal's shoes as the horse whirled and bounded out to the road toward town. Lonny stood in the drizzling rain, his arms loaded with split wood. Pa's chest heaved with heavy, hard breathing. His eyes turned slowly, returning from his thoughts. He glared at Lonny.

"Pa," Lonny said. He had nothing to say, but he said again, "Pa?"

"Git the wagon, boy," Pa ordered. "Go borrow Dan Johnson's hounds."

Aunt Louise stood in the door behind Pa. "Aren't you goin' to see Doc?" she asked, her voice strange, high-pitched.

"No," Pa said. "That cat's tracks are still hot."

Pa looked at Lonny and suddenly Pa's face twisted. "We got that cat to go git, boy. We obliged to do it." Lonny still stood, wood in his arms, water dripping from his eyebrows. "Git that wagon, boy!" Pa roared. Lonny dropped the kindling and ran to the barn.

The mule trotted over a rutted washboard road and Lonny stood in the wagon lashing the animal to greater speed. Every shadow cast by the looming trees could be Weakfoot! The screech of an ungreased axle could be the panther's cry. Don Johnson's house was a speck of light in the distance now.

Cold fingers of rain trickled down Lonny's collar, matted his hair, and dripped from his face. Beneath him the wagon slipped and clattered, skidding mud and bouncing behind the mule. From the animal's feet came a spray of wet clay which speckled Lonny's clothes, arms, and face.

"Hee-yow!" He popped the mule's rump. In the dark, he could only guess at the road ahead, giving the mule his head and hoping the wagon would remain upright.

Lonny turned the mule into the Johnson yard and jumped out of the wagon, slipping in the mud as he ran. He raced up the steps two at a time as Don Johnson opened the door. The older man's face faded from a welcoming smile as he studied the boy.

"You're drenched, kid. Come in and get warm. I'll get you something warm to wear and a hot drink."

"No!" Lonny leaned against the door with one arm. "Got to borrow your hounds! Pa wants them."

"What's wrong?"

Lonny wiped a muddy hand across his face. "Doc Manners went hunting Weakfoot and cornered him near Cramer Island. The cat clawed him up bad."

The thought made Lonny's knees weak. "Pa wants to borrow your hounds." Then, as an afterthough, Lonny added, "If you'll let us have them."

Without another word they ran to the barn and, together, chained the hounds to a leather leash. "This leash comes apart in two sections," Don Johnson said, "so you and your pa can each take three dogs."

They hauled the wagon around to face home. The rain fell harder and the sound of it on the roof of the house made Don's offer of dry clothes and something to drink more appealing. Lonny dared not pause now. Don Johnson grabbed his arm as Lonny started to climb in the wagon.

"Do you want me to go with you? It'll only take a minute to get ready."

Pa had not said, don't bring anyone. Yet Lonny knew Pa wanted to do this alone. He shook his head. "No, thanks. Pa has it worked out."

He wrapped the reins around one hand and stood in the wagon. "Gid-dap! Hee-yow, mule!" The beast leaped forward. Don Johnson's hounds scrambled to keep their balance, their toenails digging at the floorboards of the wagon. The vehicle skidded in the mud as it rounded the corner onto the main road again, the mule struggling to keep his footing. Lonny slapped the animal again and the mule strained forward.

The ride home seemed twice as long. Finally, the mule hit the last bridge. The roar of a swollen creek shot beneath Lonny, the loose planks a short burst under the wagon wheels. Pa stood on the back steps waiting, Aunt Louise above him on the porch. She had been crying and was holding her apron tightly in both hands. Pa placed his rifle and Lonny's beside the wagon seat. He handed the boy two lanterns. "Hold them," Pa instructed, "so they won't git broken."

Pa gave Lonny several cartridges.

"But Pa!" Lonny protested. "I carry more shells than this just coon hunting!"

"There's ain't but one cat, boy. There won't be time for more than two, maybe three shots." Pa climbed in the wagon and took the reins.

Aunt Louise was still standing on the porch when Lonny glanced back from the clearing down the road. Her figure was silhouetted against the light from the kitchen door. Seeing her standing there, knowing her thoughts, Lonny's guilt intensified. Should've killed that cat. I had my chance when Bay was fighting him and again when Weakfoot jumped me alone and didn't do it. Should have killed him! If I wasn't such a coward, Doc would be all right now.

"Doc dragged hisself from Cramer Island," Pa said, thinking aloud. "If Weakfoot clawed him, Doc had panther scent all over him. The hounds should pick it up and lead us to the place where Doc was attacked."

It seemed forever until Doc's house came into sight. Horses were hitched around the house, wagons stood in the yard. Neighbors had come to offer a helping hand—or perhaps to pay their respects to Doc's widow. They passed the house and Pa's features stood out in the light from Doc's windows. Pa's lips, usually smiling, or ready to smile, were two thin lines. He didn't look left or right in passing Doc's place.

Pa turned the mule off the main road through a large cornfield. The wagon's wheels mired in the mud and the mule faltered, then jerked them forward. They stopped under a magnolia tree.

"Light the lanterns," Pa said, giving Lonny dry matches. Lonny handed down the two rifles. He lit the lanterns while Pa separated the leashes. Lonny took three hounds. Pa took three. Then, by the glow of the lanterns, they spread out to search for Doc's scent and the odor of the panther.

That cat's smell is gone by now, Lonny thought. The rain washed it away.

The hounds held their noses to the ground, snorted, sniffed, sniffed, then snorted again to clear their nostrils. Don Johnson used his dogs only for big game hunting. They weren't likely to take to a rabbit, coon, or possum. Suddenly, like a cork on a fishing line, the bobbing barks plunged into full cry and Pa's dogs strained forward to follow the scent.

"Over here!" Pa yelled.

The hounds dragged them over stumps and fallen trees, through the frothing waters of swollen creeks. Slowly, foot by foot, they back-tracked the way Doc had come, dragging his body from point to point. Lonny could almost see the man stumbling, rising, and stumbling again, struggling for home and safety and comfort.

Beneath an aged persimmon tree they found the scene of battle. Four dead hounds, the clawed earth, told what it must have been like. Pa raised his lantern and turned around, his face constricted.

"Doc's favorite hounds," Pa said. His gaze fell on Lonny. "Let the dogs off the leash, Son."

The hounds jumped forward, "test-smelling" the dead dogs. In ever-widening circles they searched for the scent that would tell them which way the cat went. Lonny and Pa waited, saying nothing to one another, speaking now and then to the dogs.

"Git on it, hounds," Pa said softly. "Git on it."

The dogs milled in and around the area beneath the persimmon tree. Several minutes passed.

"They can't decide which way he went," Lonny said.

"The rain isn't helping," Pa noted.

Even as he spoke, the first low bark came. *Bar-roof!* Lonny gripped his rifle. The hound's voice rose again, more certain. The pack struck the trail and their voices lifted in melodic tones, bass and tenor, crying with the sound of the chase.

"There they go!"

Running now, Lonny and Pa followed the pack. Lanterns high, they ran through the swamp, the night parting before their lights and closing behind them. The earth firmed as they approached the glen where Bay had died under Weakfoot's slashing claws. Lonny's excitement faded to a dull throb in his stomach. I won't be afraid, he thought. His fear of being afraid grew beyond his fear of the panther.

They did not pause in the glen, but ran through matted underbrush, fighting honeysuckle and muscadine vines.

"Wait a minute!" Pa halted abruptly, listening.

The tone of the hounds' cries changed to a fever pitch. "They're on him!" Pa said, and his voice frightened Lonny. They reached a towering oak growing beside a high clay bank. A musky odor of wet hair hung heavy in the air.

"This must be the place they ran Weakfoot up," Pa said, studying the tracks in the sandy loam beneath the tree.

The hounds were at a distance. Their full-throated yelps meant the cat was running and they were hot behind. On and on they ran, to the river's edge and then doubled back again. Lonny and Pa raced after the pack, trying to catch up.

"Why don't that cat double around?" Pa growled. "Runs like he aims to go to one particular place!"

"Pa," Lonny gasped, "why don't we wait for

them to bring Weakfoot to a stand?" Pa glared at the boy.

"You saw Doc's dead dogs?"

"Yes sir."

"That's why," Pa said.

7

Weakfoot raced through the marshes, across the glen, down through Cypress Swamp. Panic drove her to greater strength and the pain in her shoulder was almost forgotten. Instinct told her the dogs would not quit. They would run and run until they ran her down and the kittens in her den beside the oak tree would starve. She was weak from her fight with the pack this morning, and the wound in her shoulder did not allow her to run as ably or as long. Weakfoot ran with a purpose, dodging, up steep banks, across dreaded waters of swift-running creeks, hoping to confuse the pack. She followed a familiar path, her black body racing through the night.

In a gnarled oak tree, deep inland, another pair of ears perked forward. Weakfoot's mate peered into the night, unblinking, listening to the far cry of a hunting pack. The safety of his den in the crotch of the tree gave the male cat satisfaction. He stirred uneasily nonetheless, and stood, his long tail twitching back and forth at the tip.

Could it be? The dogs seemed to be coming toward him, penetrating the waters of the swamp and the tangled undergrowth of vines and brush. The male cat stood motionless.

His sensitive ears detected the barest crack

of a twig and the sound of a padded foot. He gave a nervous grumble and strained to hear more. In an instant, the she cat, Weakfoot, was in the crotch of the tree with him. In a flurry of spitting and clawing, fangs bared, they fought. Weakfoot bounded higher up the tree, then out a long limb to its breaking point. She leaped to the ground and stumbled on her weak shoulder, the pain stabbing like knives down her side. She doubled back, toward her own den, toward the oncoming dogs. The male cat grumbled at this invasion of his privacy, then jerked his head around as the first hound's splashing feet came to his ears. He had been tricked! The hounds came, bellowing their hunting cry, breaking through the bramble and vines. The male cat wheeled, climbed the same limb as Weakfoot, leaped down in her tracks and ran in the opposite direction. The dogs were right behind him, almost upon his heels, as the male cat dashed away in the dark along the river bank.

Pa ran ahead and Lonny followed. They raced toward the glen once more. Lonny's heart jumped to his throat and he halted.

"Listen!" Lonny yelled.

Pa stopped. After a moment, Pa asked, "What, Lonny?"

"I—I thought I heard something run by me, over there to the left."

Pa started walking again. "Deer, maybe."

They had almost reached the glen when they stopped. "That cat's still headed the other way," Pa said calmly. "Seems like he'd turn back by now or go to his den. Must be headed for his den, otherwise he would've turned afore now."

Pa hurried on toward the glen, stooping low under overhanging limbs. Lonny turned to follow and paused as a sound came to his ears. He turned, holding his lantern high and a black body came into the clearing, veered sharply, doubled back, and disappeared into the woods.

"Weakfoot! Pa! Weakfoot!"

Pa ran back to the boy. "Where?"

Lonny pointed to the spot where the cat had emerged. Pa studied the ground by lantern light. There were tracks, all right.

"But the hounds—" Pa stood and listened. "They're goin' in the other direction!"

The baying of the dogs was so faint now the slightest breeze rustling the sawgrass left Pa and Lonny listening to nothing but the wind.

"That," Pa announced at last, "is why Weakfoot has lived so long. He's smart, old Weakfoot is. Those hounds are probably chasing a fox or a bobcat while Weakfoot goes home and takes a nap."

Lonny was surprised at the lack of bitterness in Pa's tone. "Let's go home, boy," Pa said. "Let's go see if Doc is all right. No use trying to call back those dogs with the cow horn, they wouldn't pay attention if they heard it."

"Just leave the dogs, Pa?"

Pa thought a moment. "Come back and git them tomorrow, I suppose. They're goin' to the next state and back tonight."

One lone bark made them pause. A single hound, separated from the others. "Probably that youngest redbone," Pa decided.

"I'll git him, Pa," Lonny offered.

"Careful of snakes, boy. Can you find your way?"

"Yes sir."

Lonny walked quickly, moving toward the sound of the dog. He whistled once, waited, listening, and whistled again. The dog didn't reply. The whine he'd heard a moment ago was gone.

"Come on, hound," Lonny called. "Here! Here! Here! Come on!" He raised his cow horn and blew it in a long, low tone. Complete silence. The critters of the swamp were scared to move after the bark and yelp of a pack of hunting dogs passing through. Lonny walked toward the river, lifting his lantern higher. The flame flickered and he exposed more of the wick. He held the lantern overhead and whistled again.

"Yooo, hound. Yo, yo, yo!" Lonny moved deeper into the matted muscadine and water oak area. He called again, "Yo, yo, yo!"

He bent low and peered under the same dense undergrowth as far as the lantern would let him see by its pale yellow flame. "I'm not goin' to crawl around under there at night," Lonny said aloud. "Not for that hound or any other hound!" The lantern flame sparked and yellowed, burning blue next to the wick. Lonny gave the wick another turn. He shook it and heard no sound of liquid.

I'm goin' to be in the dark in another minute, he thought angrily. He turned to go back to Pa and a movement at the edge of the light's reach made his heart leap.

Weakfoot? No—not even a beast as brave as Weakfoot would chance another encounter with the hounds. Weakfoot was most likely back in his den.

"Pa?"

Lonny thumbed the hammer of his rifle. He moved toward the tree where he saw the movement, holding his weapon waist-high, pointing it out before him.

"Pa?" Lonny called again, insistently.

He neared the tree, and as he did so the lantern flickered again. It was about to go out. Lonny moved quickly. With a sudden dash he circled the tree. He threw up the lantern and halted abruptly. Two wild yellow eyes caught the light of the lantern. A naked, bearded, mud-covered creature stared at the boy and a wiggling hound was held captive by the man. A foul odor assailed Lonny's nostrils.

"What? Who?" Lonny lifted the lantern to better see the man holding the protesting hound, one hand clamped over the dog's mouth to silence the animal. The flame of the lantern sputtered and died, letting the dark close about him.

Lonny knew he was in danger. He knew even before the man lunged in the dark. Only Lonny's leap aside saved him from the tackle. Lonny swung his rifle as he would a club. The barrel connected and the man recoiled with a grunt.

"This rifle is loaded, mister," Lonny warned. The reply to the boy's threat was not long coming. Two arms grabbed Lonny about the waist and the man's shoulder drove into the boy's midsection, driving the breath from Lonny's lungs. The man's stringy, coarse hair was in Lonny's face, and the horrible odor of the creature made Lonny gasp as they rolled together, wrestling on the soggy earth, striking trees and becoming entangled in vines.

Lonny yanked himself free. Which way to run?

"Pa!" Lonny yelled. "Pa!"

A hard blow fell across Lonny's brow and pain zig-zagged between his temples. He felt himself falling and struggled to raise his rifle but could not. Another blow, harder than the first, glanced off the boy's head. He fell face forward and his nose plowed into moist soil. His open mouth scooped sandy loam. The club came down again and this time it struck Lonny between the shoulders. The roaring in his ears rose in volume and unconsciousness overtook him.

The bellow of a bull 'gator caromed across Cramer Island. The sound faded away, the last echo a gentle murmur. A bluejay shrieked sharply, angrily, then quit. Lonny tried to turn over and could not. Every muscle was a pain in itself. His eyes felt puffed and they burned. Blood and dirt were a gritty taste in his mouth. He tried to spit it out and he couldn't make his tongue move the way he wanted it to go.

His ears buzzed and he faintly remembered the sound from somewhere before. Lonny tried to clear his mind, but the ache of his muscles became so sharp he cried aloud. He couldn't see. Panic gripped him as the thought of being blind entered his mind. The buzz in his ears was a steady hum.

The flies! The gnats and flies! Lonny recalled the insects swarming on the stolen pig he'd found while hunting Weakfoot a few days ago. Again, the boy tried to turn over and could not. His hands and feet were numb and his struggles made him gasp for breath as a noose tightened on his throat.

Hog-tied!

If he struggled to straighten his legs, the cord tying his feet to his neck would choke him. Lonny remained as still as his many discomforts would allow. Just as he decided he could not stand such agony any longer, he ebbed into unconsciousness again.

How many minutes or hours passed during the periods of sleep, Lonny could not know. He awoke time and again, his limbs throbbing from lack of circulation. He could not say whether he had been here a day, a week, or a month—or even for several short hours.

A new sound came to his ears, a snap of brittle wood.

Weakfoot!

He struggled to break his bonds, and the cord around his throat tightened unmercifully. He twisted violently, throwing himself about by arching his back. The cord became more constricting.

I'm dying now! I'm going to be dead in a minute. He stopped struggling, fear seizing him. Strangled my fool self to death, he thought. Killed myself afore Weakfoot could do it. His breath raled as he tried to suck air past the noose. His head was swimming, throbbing, and he passed out again.

8

Lonny knew his attacker was there. He could smell the beast. Rough hands untied the blindfold and Lonny blinked up into blinding sunlight. He squinted his eyes, turning his face away. The light seared his pupils and made his head hurt.

"Dunt shawt," the man warned.

Lonny peered up with eyes barely opened, not understanding.

"Dunt shawt," the man repeated.

Lonny nodded, although he had no idea what had been said. His captor removed a dirty rag crammed in Lonny's mouth. The boy coughed fitfully, jaws aching. He stuck his tongue out and raked it across his teeth trying to remove the sand still there. The man squatted, watching. The beast wore a one-piece hide across his body, like pictures of cavemen Lonny had seen. The hide hung to his thighs front and back. He wore nothing else. His red beard was bushy, snarled, filled with bits and pieces of briars and weeds. Lonny squirmed to relieve the pressure on his arms and legs.

"Please," Lonny said evenly, "untie me. I'm hurting."

The man's yellow eyes stared unblinking at

his captive. He scratched his belly with long fingernails.

"You had no call to beat me," Lonny accused.

A suggestion of a smile touched the man's parched, cracked lips. He continued scratching, squatting beside Lonny.

"Move away," Lonny demanded. "You smell bad."

The creature continued staring, kept scratching.

"How come you beat me?" Lonny asked.

"You saw—me." The man's words were so slurred the boy could barely understand them.

"You nigh killed me, you know that? What do you want, old man?"

The man rocked gently back and forth from heel to toe, his dirty hair and his odor sickening to Lonny. As the boy watched, the old man began bouncing on his haunches, up and down, pretty much as an ape might do it, Lonny decided. The old man's mouth was open and his face looked like he was laughing, but no sound came from his lips. Then as he gained momentum he suddenly sprang to his feet and a weird, strangled noise came from his throat.

"Dunt shawt," the old man said again, rolling Lonny over so roughly the boy cried aloud. The man pulled up the rope and for a moment Lonny thought the beast was going to strangle him dead here and now. The pressure released and left Lonny's wrists, neck, and ankles burning. So stiff was he, Lonny could not bring his arms from behind his back. He lay on the ground, biting his lip to hush his cries. Blood rushed through his limbs and brought a stinging pain that became unbearable, as though hundreds of needles were jabbing into his flesh. The man stood over Lonny watching. Finally, when Lonny was still, the man left for a few moments and returned with a vessel made of baked clay. He gave the boy the crude cup filled with steaming liquid. When Lonny could not hold the cup by himself, the old man grabbed the boy by the hair of his head and lifted Lonny to a sitting position.

"Ain't there a gentle bone in your stinking body?" Lonny cried. "Just keep your hands and your drinks to yourself! I got no mind to be touched by you and you make me ache all over when you yank me around like that!"

As though he hadn't heard Lonny, the old man lifted the cup to Lonny's lips and the boy was obliged to drink or have it poured on him.

Sassafras tea. Lonny closed his eyes and drank it all as quickly as possible.

The old man released Lonny's hair and let the boy lie back against the trunk of the oak tree. Lonny looked down and saw his ankles were tied to a stake driven deep into the ground. The old man squatted a few feet away and began his bouncing motion again. When he smiled, Lonny noted, only one tooth could be seen.

"Wad moor?" the old man asked.

Lonny couldn't decide whether the man had a misshaped mouth or what. The words came out as words but they made no sense. At least, Lonny couldn't understand them.

"Is that English?" Lonny asked. The question angered the old man.

"I—I can't understand you," Lonny explained.

"I done he-ar tall in thureen ye-ars."

"You what?"

The old man arose abruptly and walked away. Lonny heard his captor mumbling to himself. Then the old man returned and squatted once more.

"I don't he-ar talk in thir-teen ye-ars."

Lonny stared at the man in amazement. "You mean nobody has—nobody has talked to you for thirteen years?"

The man who was supposed to have been eaten by Weakfoot, the man wanted for murder and thought dead! Here he was! Lonny's eyes betrayed his thoughts and the old man pointed a long-nailed finger at the boy.

" Har . . . har . . . har. . . ." He jabbed his finger at Lonny. "You know!" Lonny understood him to say. "You know!"

"You're Smutt. Tom Smutt!"

The old man nodded, jumping up and down on his haunches and laughing hysterically, the gurgling sound coming in gasping, choked tones. He wagged his shaggy head like a madman.

"I'll be—" Lonny said in wonder. The amazement in the boy's manner pleased Smutt. The old man threw himself backward in a somersault, cackling uncontrollably. Smutt hopped around the camp with astounding agility and finally came back to squat beside Lonny again.

"Talk!" Smutt commanded.

"Talk about what?"

Smutt waved a hand to show he didn't care. "Talk," he repeated.

"I'll tell you this," Lonny allowed. "I got the worst beating of my life from you, last night. Was it last night?"

Smutt shook his head and flicked his fingers to show it had been several nights ago. Pa and Aunt Louise must be out of their minds with worry.

"I got to go home!" Lonny said suddenly.

Smutt stopped bouncing and glared at the boy, his yellow eyes hard and cold.

"My pa and Aunt Louise will be worried," Lonny said, reaching down to untie his ankles.

Unexpectedly, Smutt sprang upon Lonny, pushing the boy backward. Lonny cried out as the strain on his muscles brought fresh pains.

"No!" Smutt ordered. "No!"

Crazy, Lonny thought. All these years out here and he's gone crazy.

Finally Smutt allowed Lonny to sit up. Smutt demanded again, "Talk!"

Lonny talked, about Aunt Louise and how she came to live with them after Ma died nine years ago. He talked about Pa and their hunt for Weakfoot. When Smutt didn't understand the name "Weakfoot," Lonny explained about the print softer than the others because of Doc Manners' first fight with the cat. Lonny wondered, as he talked about Doc Manners, whether Doc was alive or not.

"Weakfoot," Smutt said, nodding. He knew this cat, and he knew the fear of living each night where such an animal might attack a sleeping man.

Lonny talked until his throat was parched and he could think of nothing more to say, and still Smutt commanded, "Talk!"

"I'm talked out," Lonny complained. "Let me rest myself."

Smutt fetched another crock of sassafras tea. Lonny held it, resting against the oak. He was still very much a prisoner. He watched the old man preparing food. Years of primitive living had made him a savage.

"Why didn't you kill me, Smutt?" Lonny asked. The old man bent over a battered pot, holding it over a small smokeless fire. "You could of killed me, easy," Lonny mused. "Might as well have. Wouldn't be bothered with me now. Why didn't you?"

Lonny decided to test the old man. "You were afraid to kill me?" Lonny debated aloud.

Smutt's yellow eyes became as cold as a winter pump handle as he gazed directly at the boy. Lonny shivered. Smutt was not afraid to kill, he saw that.

The old man handed Lonny a bowl of half-cooked meat.

"Because you wanted company? Is that why you brought me here alive?"

Smutt raked food from the bowl with his fingers, sucking the meal from his hand. "Maybe —maybe you ain't decided," Lonny said. He watched the hairy beast closely for a telltale reaction. "Maybe you ain't decided whether to kill me or not."

Smutt did not even glance up.

"Or maybe you have decided to kill me when you're tired of messing with me," Lonny offered.

The boy sniffed the bowl of food. "What is this?"

"Deer."

"More like possum," Lonny scoffed. Smutt chuckled, still eating.

Lonny put one finger in the hash and touched the finger to his tongue. It was almost tasteless and very greasy. His stomach twisted at the thought of eating it.

"Smutt," Lonny asked, his voice a normal, calm tone, "you plan to kill me, don't you?"

Smutt paused not even a full second, but Lonny caught that hesitation. Smutt continued eating, his movements slower, more deliberate.

"Plan to keep me around until I'm too much trouble, then kill me," Lonny concluded.

Smutt's thick red eyebrows pulled low over his eyes.

"You'd want to do it so as to make everybody think I just disappeared. Maybe like I had an accident, or got killed by Weakfoot—'gator-eaten, maybe."

Smutt rose and walked to the river's edge. The old man washed out his bowl, using sand to scrub it, water to rinse it. When he had finished, he shook the water off the bowl and returned.

"If *I* was goin' to kill me," Lonny went on, taunting the old man, "I'd make it natural, so nobody would know it was anything but an accident. Otherwise, folks would come hunting for you."

Smutt's eyes were two points of amber fire as he looked at Lonny. Lonny met the man's gaze squarely.

"I'd take a body deep into the swamp somewheres and maybe choke him to death, or drown him. You'd want to be careful not to let the body float downstream and come out of the swamp, though. Folks would find it and begin to wonder. You could cut a body up, I reckon. The 'gators and fishes would eat him sure, then."

Smutt was motionless, his eyes on Lonny. The boy wasn't sure what reaction his words were getting from the old man.

"If I was you," Lonny said, "I'd want a little company after thirteen years. Might as well! After all, it's been so long you nigh about forgot how to talk. I would want to know how everybody I ever knew was gitting along and things like that. Just as long as I didn't git in the way—you know, use me like you would a tool, until I wear out. *Then* do it."

Smutt had not moved a muscle, had not

batted an eye, listening to the rise and fall of the boy's voice and giving no indication he understood the first word.

"How you goin' to do it, Smutt?" Lonny asked.

Smutt broke his own trance and pulled at his beard, straightening the kinks and pulling out beggar's-lice.

"How you goin' to kill me, Smutt?"

Smutt's eyes returned to focus on Lonny, his face expressionless.

"Quicksand," he said.

9

The mellow note of a well-hollowed cow horn sounded over the swamp. A pack of hounds bayed, their voices rising in sweet harmony. Other horns of different tones, blown by different lips, sent low moans and high-pitched vibrations from sky to land across the bayous. There were many dogs, their yelps sharp amid the call of the horns.

Lonny awoke with a start. His wrists ached. He listened, unmoving. He heard the cow horns and hounds.

"Pa," Lonny said aloud. "It's Pa." It had to be! They were searching for Lonny. The boy's excitement dulled the burning of the cuts made in his wrists by the vines binding him. He wormed himself to a full sitting position. If he could only blow his cow horn as an answer—he felt behind himself.

Gone! He twisted around to look but the horn was not there. Had he lost it in his fight with Smutt? No, Lonny remembered having to turn over just last night to get his weight off the cow horn.

"Hee-yow!" Lonny yelled. A startled crane rose from the fog still hugging the lake's surface.

"Hee-yow!" Lonny called again. "Hoy, hoy, hoy!"

His voice came back in ebbing waves, "Oy . . . oy . . . oy. . . ."

They were coming nearer!

Smutt! Where was Smutt? Perhaps frightened away by the approaching dogs and men trampling the swamp.

Bah-oooogha! The cow horn was so near Lonny jumped.

"Hello!" Lonny cried. "Hello! Over here!"

Someone was coming, running through the brush.

"Over here!" Lonny repeated. "Under this big oak!" Tears welled in his eyes. "Hey, hey, hey! Here I am over—"

Smutt loomed over the boy, his face livid with rage. Lonny shrank as the old man raised a club.

"No!" Lonny pleaded. "I won't yell."

Smutt held the club, his eyes wild. One blow from the heavy limb would crush Lonny's skull.

"I won't yell again," Lonny vowed. "I promise."

The baying of the hounds was coming nearer and even an occasional shout between searchers could be heard. Smutt grabbed up the rag he had used to gag Lonny before. Savagely, the old man crammed the cloth into Lonny's mouth. Smutt tied the gag so tightly Lonny's mouth was forced open wide and he bit down on the gag to relieve the pressure. Then, running, Smutt went to the river and uncovered a flat-bottom boat. He threw Lonny's cow horn into the boat and shoved off, using a long pole to propel the craft.

Morning fog lingered only where the sun had not reached in pockets between woods and river mouth and under overhanging limbs shading the river banks. Lonny refused to move for fear of making his position even more uncomfortable.

Bah-oooogha! The sound was so far away only the faintest echo reached Lonny's ears. He listened intently, waiting. Finally, so far away as to be only a murmur, he heard his own cow horn again. Smutt was leading everyone deep into the swamp away from his camp and Lonny. The searchers were racing a phantom that would not be there!

With a strength born of anger, Lonny yanked up his knees, trying to pull up the stake to which his feet were tied. He twisted his arms and vines cut into his wrists.

Farther and farther away, the cow horns beckoned one another. Like a throwed calf, Lonny thought miserably. I'm helpless as a shackled heifer.

He adjusted his position so he could see the river. Across black water reflecting the blue flowers of hyacinths came the irritated chatter of squirrels and bluejays contesting one another.

I sure do need some help, God.

That didn't sound sincere. He began again. God, I'm goin' to die with redbugs and skeeter bites if something don't happen pretty quick.

He thought about his words. Maybe, maybe God just *knew* what he was trying to say. God would know things like that. Lonny thought, Please—please—

So silently did Smutt pole his swamp boat the water barely rippled around the craft. His red hair caught the sun in copper-colored hues. The muscles in his thighs and arms were thick cords undulating when he moved. The old man stood in the boat, pole raised a few inches above the water. Lonny watched him approach with the stealth of a cat, as silent as a doe and wary as a frightened rabbit.

About time! Lonny thought acidly. He was surprised at his relief upon seeing his captor return. Smutt pulled his boat onto dry land and upturned it so the bottom side would catch the sun. He laid the pole beside the craft. With practiced ease, Smutt pulled cattails and brush around the boat so even the most experienced huntsman's eye would probably pass right over it without seeing. Smutt stood on the bank watching a kingfisher dive for food. The old man scratched his abdomen with long rakes of his fingernails.

In due time, Smutt came over to the camp and squatted beside a hole where he kept the embers of a fire going at all times. He raked coals to the top and placed dry wood chips upon it, blowing gently to bring a flame without smoke.

"Hun-uh-uh," Lonny groaned insistently.

Smutt glanced around. His beard and the hair of his chest were covered with algae. A leech sucked blood from his back, below one shoulder. Smutt had obviously been in the water. The old man placed a worn saucepan over his fire and poured into it water from a jug. To this he added pieces of dried meat. He squatted, knees spread, his elbows resting on each leg, his chin on his clasped hands. He studied Lonny.

Thinking what to do with me, Lonny decided.

Smutt chewed his parched lips, his breathing heavy. Turning Lonny on his stomach, Smutt untied the gag and Lonny spit out the rag, coughing violently.

"Dunt shawt," Smutt warned, his voice hoarse.

"Don't shout?" Lonny questioned.

"Don't shout," Smutt repeated, speaking the words correctly.

"Smutt," Lonny said, "please—untie my arms."

Smutt debated, then turned the boy to one side and untied the vines from the boy's wrists. Lonny sat erect, rubbing himself, stimulating circulation. He winced when the blood began to flow freely again, making his skin burn.

"Why don't you just kill me and git it done?" Lonny asked. Smutt ignored him, returning to the fire to stir the pot of hash.

"You leave me tied here like bait for Weakfoot, or any hungry 'gator. I couldn't stop them if they were to walk up and start eating me alive."

Smutt grinned. The old man rummaged around in his lean-to. To Lonny's utter surprise, Smutt brought out a sack of sugar which he poured liberally into the hash.

"You got a leech on your back," Lonny noted calmly.

Smutt continued making the food hot.

"Want me to take it off?" Lonny asked.

Smutt reached up behind his back with one hand, feeling for the repulsive parasite. When his fingers touched it, Smutt tore it away, leaving an angry red welt. He threw the leech into the fire where it squirmed and sizzled.

The old man handed a bowl of hash to Lonny. Lonny scowled at Smutt. "Don't you ever bathe?" he asked.

Smutt cackled. "Keeps off skeeters."

"Don't have much attraction for people, either," Lonny allowed. Smutt laughed, his voice a twisted, mirthless sound. The old man concentrated on his bowl of hash, eating as before, scooping meat to his mouth and sucking his fingers.

"Smutt," Lonny said, softening his tone, "if I promise not to tell you're here, will you let me go?"

Smutt gave no indication of making a reply.

"I figure, you're not hurting anybody but

yourself out here," Lonny continued. "Stealing a little now and then, but might be I'd steal lots more if it was me."

"Eat," Smutt commanded, not looking up from his bowl.

"Way I see it," Lonny said, "being out here is punishing yourself more than any prison ever would."

Smutt wouldn't even glance at the boy.

"How about it?" Lonny questioned.

"No."

"If I give my word, on the Bible?" Lonny persisted.

"No."

"Why not?"

"You'd tell."

"Not if I swore it, I wouldn't."

Smutt continued eating.

"All right then," Lonny said, holding his voice steady, "kill me. Git it over. I'm gitting eaten alive by skeeters. Kill me, Do it today."

Smutt grinned. "Today. I do."

Smutt didn't mean to do it yet, Lonny saw that. The old man was playing with him until he wearied of his game.

"Eat," Smutt said.

Lonny tasted the greasy food and spit it out. "What a miserable way to live," he said aloud.

"Yes," Smutt agreed amiably.

"How come you don't just go on through the swamp and git away?" Lonny asked. "Go to Waycross or Brunswick, go into Florida? There ain't no call to live like—like an animal! It ain't human."

Smutt ate slowly, his eyes clouded with a fog of distant thoughts. Like a dream was the memory of a roaring fire with the fizz of a pot of coffee coming to a boil on a wood stove. He couldn't remember what it was like to have a completely dry bed when it rained, a roof overhead sheltering him from the night and the cold. He vaguely recalled the taste of fresh corn with butter melting between soft, yellow kernels. And salt! Salt on the meat. The aroma of chicken frying in deep fat—he smelled it sometimes when he dared go outside the swamp to steal a dog's pan to cook in, or sugar from an illicit whiskey still. Sometimes in his sleep he could hear bacon frying in a griddle and the quick *plop!* He remembered—no, he dared not remember—the feel of clean sheets and soft clothing. Imagine a bath in scalding hot water that covered the entire body, the smell of soap; a clean-shaven face. Clippers to pare his fingernails so they wouldn't just break off would be a luxury out here. A comb, scissors for cutting his hair, lantern light to ease the eyes when darkness fell; oh, God, to have all that. He nearly got caught the first year he ran away, trying to steal something most men never give a thought to—water. Fresh, chilled, unflavored well water instead of rain gathered after it has picked up dust and swamp odors running down a network of laced palmetto leaves which funneled the precious liquid into a jar.

Who could know, except maybe another swamp critter, the constant, never-yielding fear of living this way? Where a toothache lasted for months until he, in agony, tore out the painful molar, screaming inside but outwardly silent. A broken arm, a broken leg, if it ever happened, meant sure death. Out here, the creature that survived was the one that ran the fastest, dodged the quickest, waited the most patiently. For a man, a pitiful animal like man, all other beasts were better suited for life in the swamp. They could see what Smutt never saw, hear what he never heard, smell what his nose could not sense. The other swamp creatures had protective coloration to hide them, natural bodyguards against the elements. But Smutt, burned by sun, drenched by rain, chilled by winter, was miserably inept in all ways except one—his brain. He was smarter than any animal out here, except when another man invaded his domain. It was his wits that kept him alive. Yet when it came to the daily chores of survival, he would gladly have traded his intelligence for the eyes of an owl, the ears of a rabbit, the nose of a mouse, the speed of a deer, the fangs of a snake, or the stealth of a bobcat.

Lonny leaned forward and stared unbelieving at the old man. Smutt was motionless except for the heaving of his powerful shoulders. He squatted, two fingers poised in his bowl of hash, tears running from his eyes into the matted beard. He wept, making no sound, looking across the river toward the setting sun—remembering.

10

Search parties came every day for two weeks. The
hounds bayed and cow horns blew. If they came
too near, Smutt gagged Lonny and led the searchers deep into Cypress Swamp. Finally, a day came
when no dogs barked; no cow horns sounded.
After that, a single cow horn could be heard now
and then. Long minutes passed before the one
cow horn would call again. Lonny knew it was
Pa, still looking. Probably more to satisfy Aunt
Louise's tortured mind than for Pa's belief that
Lonny could possibly still be alive, Pa came for
three weeks, every other day, searching in vain.
Lonny listened, crying in frustration. Pa's horn
blew, sounding low and mellow but carrying for
miles, as only Pa could blow a cow horn. But Pa
couldn't continue to spend his days this way.
Finally, days passed and Pa did not come. Lonny
knew they had given up.

He heard the cow horn in late afternoon for
the last time. The sun was beginning to set and
Pa had been looking since sunup, for the first day
since over a week had passed. The swamp was
unusually quiet, the crests of trees tipped red
and gold by the setting sun. Pa had been calling
on the horn, waiting, walking, and calling again.
Lonny listened, knowing Pa's misery, and the

boy ached for his father. Lonny sat up as the gentle, smooth cow horn began the final call. He listened to the sound rising, a mellow tone that signaled day was done. It was the way a man called his hounds at the close of a hunt. Lonny knew what Pa was doing. Pa was telling his son's spirit farewell.

On and on blew the final call. On and on the note floated across Cypress Swamp. Creatures large and small paused wherever they were, listening. Pa blew the horn with a single note lasting longer than any Lonny had ever heard before, or would ever hear again. Lonny could imagine Pa with tears in his eyes, his head back so the sound carried well. It came long, soft, with feeling, and the sound of it echoed and echoed and before the final echo, Pa blew it again. Then, Lonny knew Pa would drop to his knees, spent, head bowed, to pray.

When Smutt returned from hunting, Lonny snapped, "Now they think I'm dead, just like you!"

Smutt looked at Lonny and the boy froze. The old man's expression was twisted. He had a sadness to his eyes, but a hardness as well. Lonny remained silent as Smutt prepared their meal. Lonny ate as much as he could stand, then spurned the rest. In the past, Smutt had shown a desire for news of the outside world. The old man had wanted Lonny to talk about anything so he could sit and listen. Tonight, he wanted no conversation.

"Just eat," Smutt commanded when Lonny asked him how his hunting trip had gone.

He's decided to do it for sure, Lonny thought. Goin' to kill me.

The night passed in anguish. A cold rain made Lonny toss fitfully. He dozed only to awaken, shivering violently. He heard the old man inside the lean-to turning uncomfortably from time to time. Lonny awoke later and became aware of Smutt standing over him in the predawn dark. The old man stood there so long Lonny became frightened that an attack was coming. But after a while, Smutt returned to his shelter. Lonny wrapped himself more securely in a hide Smutt had given him.

With the morning came drying sunshine. Usually, no matter how early Lonny awoke, Smutt was gone for the day, hunting or fishing. This morning when Lonny opened his eyes the old man was squatting near the campfire, warming sassafras tea.

"Morning," Lonny said.

Smutt arose abruptly and walked down to the river.

"May I have some tea?" Lonny called. *Think clearly!* Don't show fear, don't git excited. If Smutt's goin' to do it, he's goin' to do it. Be a man about it.

Smutt returned to the fire and swirled the contents of a saucepan heating there. He poured tea for Lonny and himself and put a handful of sugar in each bowl.

"Goin' to be a beautiful day," Lonny allowed. Smutt untied the boy's wrists, saying nothing. Lonny thanked him and leaned against the oak tree drinking his tea. All Lonny's efforts to bring Smutt into conversation failed. When the boy had finished drinking his tea, Smutt tied Lonny's hands behind his back again. Lonny felt a knife between his ankles and then, his feet were free.

"Stand up," Smutt commanded, lifting Lonny. The boy had not stood in so long his knees buckled and he pitched forward on his face. Smutt lifted Lonny again.

"I help," Smutt said, his voice more gentle than Lonny had ever heard it. They walked to the river and back, Lonny leaning heavily on Smutt's arm. When they stopped, they sat beside the fire.

He means to do it soon.

Smutt stirred the fire with a stick.

"You goin' to kill me today, Smutt?" Lonny asked.

Smutt nodded.

"You got no cause to kill me," Lonny reasoned. "I already told you I won't tell anybody you're here."

"You'd tell," Smutt contradicted. "You'd tell and they come get Smutt and kill Smutt."

Lonny saw the old man was close to tears over his task.

"Look—I know you don't want to kill me, Smutt. You just ain't a cold-blooded killer. You might have killed a man once, but I'm helpless, tied!"

Smutt jumped to his feet and snatched Lonny erect. He dragged the boy around the lean-to. Lonny struggled, stumbling, pleading, "Smutt, don't do it! Wait—wait—don't do it!"

Smutt hauled Lonny through knee-high palmetto fronds, the boy kicking and twisting. "Please, Smutt—I swear I won't tell. Swear it to God!"

"You'd tell," Smutt cried. "You'd tell!"

"Smutt—Smutt—for God's sake—please—"

Lonny dived face down and the old man stumbled over him. Lonny rolled away and Smutt came back at him. Lonny turned on his back and kicked, with all his strength. His feet caught Smutt in the belly and the old man doubled over. Lonny kicked, missed, and kicked again. His boot caught Smutt in the hip and the old man spun and fell. Lonny leaped up running. He threw himself through the palmettos. His legs wobbled and he tripped, frantically dragging himself up again, weakened by the days of inactivity.

Smutt screamed. The sound held a terror that made Lonny hesitate. The old man's voice rose again and the anguish of his cry stopped Lonny just beyond the camp. Lonny told himself, *Run, run fool, run!* But he did not. He forced himself to return. Smutt sat, legs spraddled, holding a cottonmouth moccasin behind the head. The serpent's fangs were imbedded in the old man's other arm.

Lonny ran to the lean-to. He found Smutt's knife beside the fire. Backing up to a tree, he pushed the knife as deeply into the trunk as his weight could make it go. Moving to and fro, he sawed the vines binding his wrists. The vine parted and Lonny grabbed the knife and ran to the old man. The moccasin slithered away. Smutt was stunned, looking at his wound. Lonny wrapped a vine above Smutt's elbow and twisted it tight.

Quickly, Lonny pierced Smutt's arm across the two fang holes. He lifted the old man's arm and sucked. He spat and sucked again, withdrawing lethal venom. Smutt groaned and fainted. The old man regained his senses as Lonny worked over him.

"Don't move," Lonny warned. He loosened the binding, massaged fresh blood toward the wound and tied the tourniquet again. Lonny struggled to lift Smutt and could not. He dragged Smutt to the lean-to. He repeated the act of loosening the vine to massage fresh blood into Smutt's swollen arm.

"Big cottonmouth," Smutt mumbled, closing his eyes. "Big snake."

"Big enough to kill a horse," Lonny commented.

Through the night, Lonny packed Smutt's wound with ashes from the fire and poured hot water over the bite to cleanse it. Smutt was not going to die, Lonny decided before dawn. The old man's breathing, which had become shallow and irregular soon after the snake struck him, was now steady and stronger. The racking chills and nausea had subsided.

Dawn over Cypress Swamp was more beautiful than Lonny had seen it in weeks. He strolled along the river and threw in a rock just to make frogs leap into the smooth black surface of the water. The boy found his rifle still loaded and unfired in the back of Smutt's lean-to. He took the old man's boat and poled across the lake, watching cattails for a revealing movement. When he saw it, one shot brought down a buck seeking to quench a morning thirst. Lonny managed to load the deer into the boat and poled back to camp, careful not to swamp the overloaded craft. When Smutt awoke, Lonny was skinning the deer and preparing to cure the meat.

"Morning," Lonny said cheerfully.

Smutt blinked his eyes, staring at the buck. Lonny peeled hide from the venison, gutted the animal, and removed the liver. He scoured a saucepan and fried the liver, serving it up to Smutt diced to bite-size. Smutt sniffed it suspiciously, tasted it, then eagerly ate it.

"I'm not much at cooking," Lonny admitted. "But after the blood you lost, liver is what you need. There's plenty—eat all you can while it's hot."

Lonny boiled the rag Smutt had used to gag him and made a bandage for the old man's arm.

He fashioned a sling from a thick honeysuckle vine.

"Reckon—reckon maybe I'll live," Smutt said, and Lonny wasn't sure whether it was a statement or a question.

"I reckon you'll live," Lonny agreed.

"Too bad," Smutt said.

Lonny studied the old man and continued dressing the wound. Gently, he wrapped it.

"Why'd you come back, boy?" Smutt asked.

Lonny had asked himself the same question. "I don't know. I reckon maybe I ain't a killer, either."

Smutt turned his head aside and closed his eyes tightly. "I'm a old fool," Smutt rasped.

Lonny completed Smutt's bandage and stirred the fire. In a few days Smutt would be better. Then Lonny would go home. He wondered what Aunt Louise, Pa, everyone would say. More—he wondered how he would explain his absence.

11

It was now Smutt who remained in camp as Lonny went forth to hunt and fish. The boy learned, with Smutt teaching. He built traps for snaring duck and a crude net of palmetto leaves for dipping fish.

The old man wasted nothing. He used the hide of a buck for clothing and cover, the meat to eat, the entrails as bait to trap coon and possum. Smutt took the ribs for cage bars to hold live birds and cooked the deer hooves to a thick paste he applied to chigger bites to smother the redbugs. Lonny followed the old man's example and jealously tended the fire, ever mindful not to lose their precious heat. Smutt had banked the fire each morning, wrapping coals in moss and sprinkling the embers with enough sand to keep it from blazing. At night, when the fire seemed destined to die, Smutt dug into the smoldering cinders and blew the sparks to life again.

When Lonny's lips cracked from sun exposure, Smutt counseled, "Use wax from your ears to make them well."

Smutt showed Lonny a bank of smelly mud which they applied to their arms and faces to ward off insects. Like Smutt, Lonny soon discovered that a bath invited attacks from mosquitoes and gnats. Taking to the water became less inviting.

Their bellies filled, the day over, Lonny sat beside a faintly glowing fire each evening listening to the old man talk about people now dead and times long past.

"Used to," Smutt said, his voice distant, "we didn't have lanterns. We used lighter knots from pine trees. The best ones were the ones where pitch is rising and the limb is dead. Pitch comes to a tree like blood to a man, to clean a wound and keep out disease. A good lighter knot burns bright. You got to have good light for frog gigging and 'gator hunting."

The old man's mind wandered and his words didn't always make sense, but Lonny listened. For the first time in thirteen years there were ears to hear, and Smutt talked of things like "barrel staves" and "guava jelly," which he'd forgotten how to say.

The suffering Smutt endured from the snake bite made the old man shiver one minute and an hour later be begging for water. Most of it he took in silence, complaining only if Lonny asked.

"You looking after me, ain't you, boy?" Smutt once remarked.

Each morning, going home was the first thing Lonny considered and each night it was his last thought before falling into an exhausted sleep. He could run, any minute he could run. But once home, Lonny could not easily come back without arousing questions. He would have to abandon the weak and vulnerable old man, leaving him very likely to die. Aunt Louise and Pa thought Lonny dead. Until Smutt was well enough to care for himself again, it was best left that way. When he went, Lonny knew, he would be a long time coming back, if ever.

But he did think about it. He did worry about

Aunt Louise, who was surely grieving, and Pa. After his mother died, Lonny faintly remembered, Pa sat for days without stirring, except when forced to do so. If it hadn't been for Aunt Louise, herself a widow without child, Pa might have shriveled like a rootless plant. Aunt Louise took Lonny out and presented the boy to his father.

"Consider him, then," Lonny remembered Aunt Louise saying. "If you got no cause to think of your own life, think of your son."

So far as Pa knew, today he had no son. Lonny worried. Still and yet, he could not forsake Tom Smutt. To do so would pain his mind forever, more so even than causing Pa and Aunt Louise a longer suffering. So he stayed.

Fever in the swamp is a daily threat. Water from the murky river accidentally swallowed, the bite of a certain insect, the scratch of a particular thorn—any of them might have caused it. The fever came in the night. Lonny awoke, teeth chattering, his body quaking. His clothing, tattered from lack of daily change, was soaked in perspiration. His chills alternated to fevers that made his mind think crazy thoughts, and his eyes saw things that were not there. He vomited until the muscles in his stomach ached constantly.

Lonny called out, "Smutt! Smutt!" and the old man scrambled out of the lean-to.

"I'm about to freeze!"

Smutt spread a hide smelling of sweat and wet hair over the boy. Lonny called for more cover and the old man dragged the boy nearer the fire, stoking it to greater heat with chips, unmindful of the increasing glow.

"I'm still cold," Lonny pleaded.

Lonny heard a roll of thunder and the horizon flashed with zigzags of static electricity. "Goin' to storm," Lonny said, or did he think it? The fire was roaring now, heat striking Lonny's face and chest. He had used his shirt to make bandages for Smutt's arm. The heat of fever, rising, rising, overcame his chills until Lonny threw aside the hide and exposed his body to the still night air. The old man watched the boy writhe and made no move to hush Lonny's delirious cries.

Thunder drummed a gentle song in the distance and lightning kept time. Brilliant streaks of jagged light pierced a sky growing pale blue and sharp green. So humid was the air, beads of moisture collected even on the bark of trees. Birds rose nervously from their roosts, circled, and settled again, only to rise once more as their hollow bones expanded with the dropping air pressure.

Heat mounting in Lonny's body opened every pore. His tongue was puffed and dry. Smutt lifted the boy to pour tea between Lonny's lips and the boy could not swallow it. The throbbing in Lonny's brain came and went, rendering him senseless and causing delusions. He thought he saw Aunt Louise standing at the edge of the camp.

"Aunt Louise! Come here—come here!" he begged. Her vision wavered. "Aunt Louise, please —help me—please, Aunt Louise—come here."

When he next awoke, the storm was overhead and lightning crashed like cannons. He was cold again.

"Smutt. I'm cold."

Smutt wrapped Lonny in a deer hide and Lonny threw it aside angrily. "Build up the fire, old man! I'm cold!"

Smutt wrapped him in the hide again and stirred the fire, throwing on fresh kindling. Lonny did not notice the mounting fear in Smutt's yellow eyes. The old man looked skyward as black clouds rolled thicker and higher. *Caaa-rachett!*

Lightning struck a cypress, rending the bark, peeling wood from the trunk. The tree sparked and glowed, fizzled and cooled. Smutt took down the side of deer Lonny had slain. By now, Lonny was delirious again. Smutt touched the boy's forehead and withdrew his hand, trembling.

Rain fell wind-driven, each drop stinging like grains of flying sand. Smutt wrapped Lonny in the hide as best he could. He bound the boy's arms to better hold him, and ran from the shelter. The river was rising rapidly in the deluge of rain. Already water was licking at the lean-to, and the normally placid river was a rush of swirling waters. Smutt had been so busy with Lonny, he'd allowed the boat to get swept away. Lonny dimly realized he was being carried through the underbrush by the panting old man.

"I'm cold," Lonny protested. "Cover me, I'm cold!"

Smutt gasped from the exertion of carrying the boy's weight. He hugged Lonny to his chest. The deer hide dropped and Smutt rushed on without it. When Lonny awoke again he was in water —Smutt was chest-deep in a swift-running stream. Lonny collapsed against the hairy chest and Smutt's muscles tightened as he stumbled, caught himself, and climbed free of the sucking stream.

Lonny opened his eyes to see a bolt of lightning shimmering overhead. In the split-second of birth, the bolt formed, darted, and delivered an ear-splitting crash that struck a tree not thirty yards away, enveloping the trunk in flames. The air was filled with an odor like flint upon flint. Smutt tripped, and dully Lonny wondered if the old man could make it to his feet again. Smutt grunted with the strain, lifting Lonny, his legs quivering under the weight. The rain made Lonny slippery to hold, and Smutt's snake-bitten arm was a constant pain to the old man. Lonny heard him sucking air between groans.

It seemed hours that they pushed through the dark, fighting the whine of wind and the pelt of rain, being whipped by the howling storm. Smutt staggered onward, ever slower, sinking in bogs, skirting swollen streams.

In his fever-ridden mind, Lonny heard Pa's voice saying, "Come on, boy—don't do old Bay like that!"

He could see himself looking down at the hound and heard his own voice saying, "Did you think I was goin' somewhere? Did you think I'd take a no-good hound like you hunting?" The dog's reply, a happy *bar-roof!*

The image faded with Pa's booming laughter. Lonny awoke screaming, "Pa! Pa! Pa!"

"Easy, boy," Smutt soothed him. "Easy—easy now."

They reached firm going and high ground and the old man lowered Lonny gently to the earth, shielding Lonny's face and chest with his own body. The heaven's anger knew no mercy. Piercing shrieks of wind in the trees sounded like a thousand voices wailing. Lonny shivered with chills and gasped in the fever that followed.

He awoke with Smutt's arms crushing the breath from his lungs, so tight was the old man's hold on him. Lonny felt something slapping his face and he twisted slightly to see what was happening. Corn? Cornstalks striking his face! Lonny began crying. He tried to stop himself and could not. His voice was lost in the screeching wind. In a flash of lightning he saw a familiar outline— the barn!

Smutt labored to mount the split-rail fence

and upon reaching the other side, he slipped in the mud and fell flat on his back with Lonny atop his chest. The boy heard the breath go from Smutt's lungs. Crying hysterically, Lonny rolled off the old man's motionless body. He crawled on all fours, water racing across his hands and between his knees as it flowed over the clay yard in red rivulets. Lonny fell face forward and it took a supreme effort to rise on all fours again. Bursts of lightning showed him the way. He heard his own voice, a weak protest against the howling elements. He shouted, "Pa-aaaa!" But no more than a whisper reached his own ears—nobody could hear him in the din of the storm.

Wind caught the shutters of the house and rattled them. Shingles on the roof peeled away before the awesome wind. A churn flew across the yard, slammed the barn, and bounced like a child's rubber ball. It was dashed upon a fence stanchion, splintering, the pieces flying away in the dark. The rain drove with such force Lonny's flesh burned as though pricked by thousands of needle points. He reached the steps, clawing his way up, one at a time, holding each board to keep from being blown into the yard again.

"Pa-aaaa!" He screamed as loud as he could. To a grieving man and woman, such sounds come even on a still night. They could not brave a storm to see what they already knew—nobody could be out there.

Splinters snagged Lonny's nails, tore his fingers, but he did not feel it. He fell on his stomach, clinging to the cracks of the porch, pulling himself toward the door. The house creaked, shifting, and settling. Lonny put his face to the bottom of the door. Rags had been pushed against it from the inside to soak up water that had been blowing through.

"Paaa-aaa!" He pushed against the door, banging it feebly with his fists. "Paaa-aaa!"

Aunt Louise rocked, sitting beside the fireplace, knitting by the light of a single kerosene lamp. Pa sat across from her, reading. The wind was a constant roar, and occasionally it caused a back draft and made smoke choke in the chimney, belching soot into the room. Pa adjusted the damper and sat down again. They said very little to one another these days. They seldom let their eyes meet.

Suddenly, Aunt Louise stiffened her back, halting the rocking chair. Pa noticed, but pretended to continue reading. Aunt Louise sat, head high, very still, almost not breathing. As though Pa read her mind, he said, "Just the wind, Louise."

She nodded, sitting back, and lifted her knitting needles with trembling hands. But she noticed Pa turn his head slightly, his eyes no longer seeing the words on the pages of the book he held. Aunt Louise dropped a needle to the floor and she and her brother stared at one another. For a moment they would not admit, could not dare to believe, that they had heard anything. They waited, waited, waited, waited.

"Paaaaa-aaaaa—" The wind. Nothing more. They were asking for a new hurt of an old wound. It was foolish to fancy that it was anything other than the storm and an aching desire making their minds play tricks with their hearts. Still, Pa and Aunt Louise were not moving, looking at one another.

"Paaaa-aaaa—"

Aunt Louise's lips twisted and she lifted the back of one hand to her mouth. "Oh, God—" she whispered.

Pa lunged at the door. He lifted a heavy beam and threw it aside. The wind slammed open the door and curtains in the farthest bedroom swirled, the fire leaping up the chimney, flames snapping angrily.

Lonny pitched forward and fell between Pa's legs. Far away, screaming and crying, he could hear Aunt Louise. Powerful arms lifted him. Lonny dimly smelled the room, the warmth of it, felt the hands touching him and heard them crying, Aunt Louise and Pa. A dream again? Another delusion?

"Cold. . . ."

". . . fever. . . ."

"God—thank God."

"Bed."

". . . thank . . . God . . . fever . . . dry clothes . . . is he all right?"

Darkness came on Lonny again. He did not feel the sheets being pulled up around him, the hands feeling for broken bones and touching to be sure it was he and he was really there. He did not see Aunt Louise and Pa, holding one another, each of them crying, reaching out now and again to touch the boy, to be absolutely sure he was really there.

The cornshuck mattress rustled, comforting, warm, and Lonny sighed heavily. Outside, in the slashing rain, a lone figure crawled through the whipped cornfield, dragging himself back to the swamps.

12

How long the storm lasted, Lonny did not know.
He vaguely remembered Pa putting chickens into
the attic and bringing their livestock into the
house. He remembered the wind, the groan of
the house straining on its moorings. The water,
he remembered that—Aunt Louise and Pa walked
barefoot because the water had risen and come
through the floor.

When the storm subsided Lonny looked
through his shuttered window. The yard was a
river and the house a high point in its swift cur-
rents. Along the fence, barely above water, snakes
by the hundreds hung on the top rail. Moccasins
and copperheads, water snakes and all that grew
and lived in the swamp, seeking high ground and
safety. The rain-beaten cornfield was a lake of
muddy, red water.

Having seen what the window allowed, too
exhausted to do more than sip a few teaspoons of
soup, Lonny fell back and slept. Doc Manners,
rowing in a boat and often spending the night,
came and sat beside Lonny for hours at a time.
"You're alive!" Lonny said. Doc nodded. Pa told
Lonny later, for seven days and eight nights the
boy slept, mumbling in his delirium, crying out
and sometimes pulling away from them. In his

senseless state, Lonny sometimes smiled and cried at the same moment.

When Lonny awoke free of the fever, the storm had passed and the water retreated, leaving a muddy mark as high as the boy's shoulder on the barn. Aunt Louise came beside the bed and looked down at Lonny. He stared at her to be sure she was really there. He struggled to raise himself, to reach for her, and she knelt, holding his hand.

"Aunt Louise?"

She studied him closely.

"Aunt Louise?" he repeated. Suddenly, seeing that this was not the fever talking, she threw herself across him, holding him, crying. Lonny put his arms around her and weakly, he held her.

"Aunt Louise," he said, with assurance. He patted her back with the tips of his fingers, closing his eyes and sleeping a sound, restful sleep he had not known since Smutt attacked him nearly three months ago.

People came from four counties away, everybody who knew Lonny, or Pa, or Aunt Louise. Doc Manners came every day and felt Lonny's forehead, mashing the boy's belly and poking pills down Lonny's throat. Folks Lonny had never really known, but had seen at county fairs and special church meetings, came to see a living miracle. Bucky Landers came with his three brothers, Ma Landers, and Shirley. Bucky gave Lonny the best puppy by his favorite redbone hound.

Nobody asked Lonny to prove how he lived through his weeks in the swamp. The fact he was alive was proof enough. Nobody asked him what he had eaten—he obviously ate enough. They didn't question Lonny about 'gators or Weakfoot or quicksand. They just looked at him and smiled and shook Pa's hand like Pa had made a personal deal with God Himself.

Aunt Louise just wanted to sit beside the boy, touching his face and holding his hand. She cried a lot during those first days after Lonny regained his own mind and his fever was gone for good. Lonny kept the puppy Bucky had given him right on the bed and Aunt Louise didn't say the first word about it. The nights of misery, the days of terror, the storm and Smutt were like dreams. Bad dreams partly, good dreams some.

Doc Manners made Lonny roll on his stomach and thumped Lonny's back.

"Yep," Doc stated, "he's fit as a fiddle and ready to play!"

Aunt Louise laughed.

"Reckon he'll be good enough in a day or two to take a hand at mud-scraping?" Pa asked Doc.

Doc nodded, winking at Lonny. "I'd say, so long as he's given plenty time to sip well water and go hunting every day or two—he could scrape mud now and then."

"If he's well then," Aunt Louise said, making her face a frown, "he'll be obliged to get that hound off the bed!"

Doc shook his head as Pa and Lonny laughed. "I don't know whether he's that well or not," Doc said.

Doc and Pa went into the kitchen and Aunt Louise served up hot coffee.

"God's will," Pa said, referring to Lonny's return.

"Just in time, too," Doc agreed. "Nothing could have lived through the hurricane out there in that swamp—nothing!"

Lonny sat up, listening.

"They say the river is full of dead hogs, cattle, deer, wild boar—all manner of animals," Doc continued. He added with a grunt, "Except Weak-foot! No sign of a cat, yet."

Lonny listened with tears in his eyes as Doc said, "Water was marked nine feet high, judging by mud left on the trunks of trees. Worst storm in eighty years, folks are saying."

Lonny swung his legs off the bed and his head hummed. He fell back until the room stopped spinning. He was too spent to try going into the kitchen. Smutt's got to be dead, Lonny thought. He couldn't have lived. Drowned, most likely.

Still, hadn't the old man done the impossible? Hadn't he lived in the heart of the swamp, snake-fighting and 'gator-wary, catching his food the best he could and stealing all else he needed? If Smutt had lived thirteen years out there without dying or getting killed, maybe nothing could kill him. As soon as his strength returned, Lonny decided, he would go search for the old man and, if he found him, take Smutt salt and a new sauce-pan and a good knife.

"I'll wager," Doc's voice came from the kitchen, "no man could've lived through that hurricane without shelter and high ground. Everything that could climb a tree did it and them that couldn't were swimming. Unless a critter could swim for three days he drowned, and his body is goin' to sea right this minute, down the St. Mary's River!"

Poor Smutt—poor, crazy old man.

For several days they would not allow Lonny to walk farther than the kitchen table. If the boy wobbled, back to bed he went.

"Swamp fever," Pa had called Lonny's sickness. It came from drinking bad water.

In due time, Lonny was permitted on the back

porch where he sat for long hours, thinking. Cool weather was upon them and Lonny wore a jacket, sitting in a rocking chair looking at the leaves of poplar and oak trees turning from green to yellow and rust. He spent his time mostly playing with the big-footed redbone puppy. In the kitchen, Aunt Louise hummed and sang to herself as she cooked.

"What you goin' to call the pup?"

Lonny jumped as if he had been shot. Shirley Landers stood at the end of the porch, grinning.

"Don't know," Lonny said. "Bay, maybe."

Shirley came around to the steps. "Wasn't that the name of your other dog? Bay?"

"Yes. Maybe Bay Jr. then, and call him Bay for short."

Shirley laughed. "I reckon you just like the name of Bay."

"I want to honor my dog," Lonny said, his voice soft.

Shirley nodded. "That'd be a good thing to do—honor Bay by calling another after his name."

Lonny was pleased she agreed with him. He discovered himself smiling and he hated the shy twist of his own lips. He made his face stern.

"Looks like a pretty good hound," Lonny said of the puppy. "It—was nice of Bucky to give him to me."

Shirley threw back her head, her laughter so sudden Pa turned from wood chopping down at the barn.

"Bucky *had* to bring you that pup," Shirley explained. "Else, how could he come and see you and still be keeping his pride?"

"See me?" Lonny questioned, knowing full well what she meant.

"See you," Shirley stated. "You're goin' to be

a legend, Lonny Bascombe, and you know it. More folks speak your name in a day than will call mine in a hundred years!"

Lonny pretended not to understand.

"Already they tell how you wrestled Weak-foot with one breath and ate bugs and bird eggs with the next."

Lonny's face mirrored his revulsion at the idea of eating bugs and bird eggs and again, Shirley laughed. Pa came onto the porch, his brawny arms loaded with kindling.

"Looks like you're the best medicine in the country," Pa said by way of greeting Shirley. "Nothing else has put such a light in the boy's eyes like your laughter."

Pa passed on through and Lonny heard the kindling as Pa dropped it into the wood box behind the stove. He stole a glance at Shirley and she was silent, looking at her hands.

"Pa—he doesn't mean to make you uneasy," Lonny explained. "He just—"

Shirley interrupted him with a wave of her fingers. "I know."

"I'm pleased you came over," Lonny blurted. "I was wishing—somebody would come over."

Shirley looked up and a smile played at the corners of her lips. "Good!" she teased. "Next time I'll send Bucky since just—*anybody* will do for company."

Lonny opened his mouth to explain, knowing she needed no explanation, and Shirley's laughter tickled the air again. She ran across the yard and rounded the house, cutting through the cornfield toward home. Aunt Louise came to the door behind Lonny.

"I was about to ask her for supper," Aunt Louise said.

"Maybe tomorrow night," Lonny said, smiling

foolishly. "Maybe she'll come back tomorrow and stay for supper."

Lonny turned and Aunt Louise was looking at him with a quizzical expression. When his eyes met hers, Aunt Louise looked away, quickly. Then she laughed, a funny little laugh, and Lonny knew she had read the look on his face. He began to redden as she looked at him again, and again she laughed.

"Shirley is a nice little—little girl," Lonny said, roughly.

Aunt Louise howled with laughter at Lonny's use of the word "little."

"Oh, sure," Aunt Louise said finally, wiping tears from her eyes with her apron. "Shirley's a nice little girl."

She didn't give Lonny a chance to think of more to say. Aunt Louise returned to the kitchen, and now and then he heard her burst into renewed laughter, her voice a sound of happiness Pa and Lonny hadn't heard in years, if ever at all.

"What's the matter with you, Louise?" Pa asked, smiling uncertainly.

"Nothing!" She stirred supper. "Just laughing about that nice little—" She was laughing so hard now she had to sit down, wiping her eyes free of tears.

"She's laughing on account of my being so stupid," Lonny stated to Pa. "I had lanterns in my eyes and she saw the light, I reckon."

Aunt Louise put her hand on Lonny's shoulder, her eyes water-filled and her face going soft as they gazed at one another.

"Good to have you home, boy," Aunt Louise said. Then she completely stunned Lonny by suddenly beginning to cry.

"Sure is," Lonny agreed. "Mighty good to be home."

Pa was watching, saying nothing. Aunt Louise slowly pulled Lonny to her and hugged him, crying softly and laughing all at the same time.

Supper was eaten that night as if it were a special holiday. They laughed at everything, Pa, Aunt Louise, and Lonny. Now and again, Aunt Louise would reach over and put her hand on Lonny's arm, or touch his hand. Her face glowed, and she had a peacefulness in her eyes that neither Pa nor Lonny had ever witnessed before.

After Lonny was in bed and the lantern had been extinguished, Aunt Louise came into his room and sat on the side of his bed. For a long time, she said nothing. She was not touching him, although he could feel her eyes on him in the dark.

"I reckon it was God who sent you to me," Aunt Louise said, softly.

"No ma'am," Lonny said. "It was God sent you to *me*."

Hesitantly, she reached over and took his hand, shy like, almost as though afraid he would pull away. Lonny met the pressure of the fingers equally.

"I'm a mite late confessing it," Aunt Louise said, her voice almost a whisper, "but I love you, boy. More than life itself, I love you."

Lonny's voice choked as he rose to hug her. "Yes ma'am," he said. "I know."

13

Aunt Louise could not hide the fear in her eyes. She repeated Lonny's woods, "Goin' hunting?"

"Yes ma'am," Lonny said. "I've finished my chores."

Pa and Lonny knew Aunt Louise was afraid for the boy, afraid to gamble on losing him in Cypress Swamp again.

"Just be careful, Son," Pa said, making it sound like a request, not an order.

"I will, Pa."

Lonny borrowed Pa's cow horn and rifle—his own had been lost at Smutt's camp. The boy vaulted the fence and walked through twisted stalks and muddy furrows. He looked back to be sure no one was watching, and retrieved a gunnysack he had hidden. He ran on into the swamp. In the sack were a saucepan, two bowls, a spoon, and a knife, as well as a fork. Fresh baked bread he'd taken from the breakfast table was wrapped in a clean cheesecloth, and in a jar were two pounds of real coffee. Things Smutt dreamed about—enough salt for six months, fried bacon rinds, and butter for the bread. Lonny could imagine Smutt's pleasure when the old man saw, smelled, tasted the food.

Lonny hurried, not pausing to consider the

muck he was getting on his trousers as he crawled through a tunnel of matted undergrowth, now slimy from the flood. He broke into the stand of cypress trees and ran to the river's edge. He had to detour around the angry, gurgling river, which still carried receding waters to the sea.

There! The oak! Lonny hurried, his mounting anticipation making him smile. The oak stood solid and unyielding, even to a storm as wrathful as the hurricane. Beneath the oak, the lean-to was gone. Beyond, where the boat had been, high water covered the cattails and sawgrass. Black mud, slippery and foul-smelling, covered the campsite.

Lonny walked slowly, horrified with thoughts of what must have unfolded here when the old man was caught by the elements. The watermark on the oak showed the river had gone three hands higher than Lonny could reach.

"Smutt!" Lonny yelled. The growling river absorbed the sound of his voice and there was no echo this day. Lonny circled the quicksand that guarded the camp's rear and he called again, "Smutt!"

He lifted his cow horn and blew it in six short blasts. They had no prearranged signal, he and the old man. Lonny lifted his sack of stores and turned full circle, showing the old man he was leaving it, if Smutt were watching. Lonny tied the sack to a vine hanging from the oak, making sure it was high enough to keep it away from any land animals. If the sack hung there long enough, coons and possums would climb the tree and down the vine, and steal the contents. There wasn't much hope that Smutt would get the gunnysack and food.

He's dead, Lonny thought. He remembered Doc's conversation a few days after the storm.

"Nothing could've lived through the hurricane out there in that swamp—nothing!"

Lonny walked to the river. He could imagine the old man, one arm snake-bitten and weak, his energy spent from carrying Lonny. The boy closed his eyes, his thoughts tormenting him.

The crack of a twig, the rustle of disturbed bramble made Lonny turn his head to listen. There, it came again.

"Smutt!" Lonny ran toward the sound. "Smutt, are you there?"

He halted, stunned.

"Hello, Lonny," Shirley Landers said. Her hair was twisted and briars clung to her dress. "I—I followed you," she admitted. "I saw you leave the house and I followed you."

Lonny turned away from her to shield his distress.

"Are you mad?" she asked. "About me following along?"

"No."

She stood beside him. "Lonny?"

"What?"

"I heard you—calling for him."

Lonny kept his back to her. He could not deny it. Any half-deaf fool would have heard him bellowing.

"I heard you calling Tom Smutt," Shirley said.

"I was calling my dog," Lonny lied. "I was saying *mutt*—here, *mutt!*"

She didn't believe him, he could see that. She studied his face and he forced himself to meet her eyes steadily. Suddenly, she whirled and laughed, looking across the river. Lonny watched her. She laughed again, a laugh too forced to be genuine.

"I never have been this far into the swamp

afore." she said. "It's exciting and scarey, isn't it?"

He made no move to reply, watching her walk to the river. "What did you do with the sack?" she asked. The unexpected turn made Lonny stammer.

"Set a coon trap—that's what was in the sack."

Shirley looked into his eyes, her face completely sober. She raised the back of one hand to her forehead and brushed hair from her face.

"I was goin' by your place to invite you to come to mine," Shirley said, her expression unchanged. "Ma says she'd be obliged to have you for supper. Nothing special, but you're welcome to eat what we got."

Lonny nodded. "I'd like that."

"Tonight?"

He nodded again.

They walked away, Lonny leading Shirley from the hanging sack. They turned toward home.

"It's a wonder you didn't git 'gator-bit," Lonny offered. Shirley noted the markings of an alligator that had slithered and crawled across the floor of the swamp.

"You like to have lost me once," she said. "When you went through that tunnel back there."

"It ain't safe to go running around out here like this," Lonny offered.

"You just goin' to leave your hound?" Shirley asked casually. Lonny knew she was on to his lies, but he had no choice but to continue lying.

"He's a smart hound. He'll git home."

They pushed through the thicket and Shirley bloused her skirt, tucking it around her legs. Lonny turned away, red-faced.

"It's sure you got no sisters," Shirley laughed.

"I do this, or take a whopping when I git home with a muddy dress."

Lonny crawled through the thick underbrush and Shirley followed, laughing at his discomfort over her lack of modesty. "I bet you never kissed a girl," Shirley teased. Lonny crawled faster.

Shirley's laugher taunted him. "Most likely, kissing a girl won't be like kissing your aunt, you know."

They reached the glen and Lonny turned angrily. "Don't tease me," he snapped. Shirley's smile vanished.

"I tease only folks I like," she said softly. "If a man be teased, he knows he's liked—a lot."

She turned up her face, moving closer to him and Lonny reached for her without thinking. Her body was soft and firm all at the same time and her warmth made him conscious of her touching him. His heart thumped, thumped, thumped and his breath came quick and sharp. He kissed her and he knew it was clumsy, tight-lipped, and too rough. She winced slightly as he squeezed her, but she did not complain. When he pulled away, she was trembling and her trembling made him shiver too.

"Supper will be close to dark, a little after," Shirley said.

He released her. "I'll be there."

Pa winked at Aunt Louise and they grinned when Lonny told them he wanted to go to the Landers home for the evening meal.

"The boy is goin' to be grown afore we know it," Pa said, meaning his words to reach Lonny's ears. "Any man who can live by his wits in Cypress Swamp for so long most likely can handle hisself with a girl," Pa added. Lonny stood in his bedroom. He started to protest and decided it would be unlike a man to deny a thing like that. He felt good suddenly, like he could run a mile at top speed. He heard Aunt Louise say, "Wash you ears, Lonny," and he smiled that she would remind him of what he had already reminded himself.

He went through his chores faster than ever before. The chickens clucked sweeter, the wind was crisper and cooler, the night clearer, the land more beautiful. He didn't even become angry when the chickens stepped in their feed trough and spilled the feed.

"Looks like the boy got hisself a girl," Pa allowed.

Lonny followed a path to Millpond, winding between hundred-year-old oaks. It was dark when he arrived at the Landers home. Their hounds rose from dust beds and hollows scooped under the back porch. Being the good hunting dogs they were, they knew Lonny was approaching and sounded a warning when the boy was fifty yards away.

"Howdy out there!" a man's voice boomed.

"Howdy!" Lonny reponded. "It's Lonny Bascombe!"

Ma Landers and her four grown sons stood on the porch with Shirley among them like a flower among thistle. The hounds bounded up to Lonny, jumping on his legs, slobbering on him.

"Git them hounds away!" Ma Landers commanded and each boy called to his own.

"Hee-uh, hee-uh, Dynamite, Lulu, Maybelle, Spots, Tinker, Tinker Too, Charlie, Snoot, Polly, and Rufus! Hee-uh! Hee-uh! Better git hee-uh, now!"

Twice widowed, Ma Landers had the work

of a man to do and she somehow did it. She could last as long as any man doing field work and she was fiercely competitive. She was respected as a lady, but handled her boys as a man would. She was known to belt her sons when the need arose. "When Ma Landers roars," Pa once said, "everything in Cypress Swamp whimpers."

Bucky greeted Lonny, "Shirley tells me that redbone hound pup'ss looking good."

"He is that," Lonny agreed.

"He wass the besst of the litter," Bucky reminded him, and Lonny wisely bragged on Bay, telling how the pup had more sense than a hound had a right to have and already he got the "hunting wiggles" and went to sniffing the air when somebody lifted a rifle. Bucky and the other brothers "shined like a noonday sun," and they told themselves what good hounds they raised.

"All right," Ma Landers ordered, "Lonny come to eat, not talk; let's eat!"

Lonny sat at the table and Shirley took the seat next to him and Ma Landers sat at the head of the table. Bucky sat across from Lonny and Shirley and Washington. Big Bob and Morton glared at Lonny and opined that their guest wasn't goin to be as big as his pa.

"All right now," Ma Landers stated, "time for the blessing!"

She began, "God, we appreciate the food. Many thanks. Amen."

Upon "Amen," arms flew across the table and forks jabbed into fist-sized biscuits and snatched the bowl of black-eye peas. Ma Landers dished up stew.

"Wait a minute!" Ma commanded. "Wait a blessed minute!"

The uproar of snatching and shouting continued. Ma took a swat at a beefy hand with a wooden ladle and demanded again, "Wait a minute!" Morton withdrew his hand, shaking it like it was covered with hot grits. They looked at Ma.

"I told you twenty times today," Ma seethed, "git that hog outten under this table afore supper."

Big Bob arose, politely excused himself, and got a shotgun from the wall. He poured a handful of salt down the barrel into an empty shell. Ma moved aside as Bob pointed the gun under the table. Lonny lunged backward, pulling up his legs as a blast of the shotgun shook the room. The table lurched, and squealing cries proved the salt had found its mark. The hog tore out Ma Landers' end of the table, knocking her chair askew. The beast raced across the room and out the back door as Big Bob hung the weapon on its pegs. He came and sat and Lonny climbed up off the floor. Everyone looked at Ma for the signal.

"Git it," Ma said and instantly the hands began flying.

"Help yourself, Bascombe!" Ma shouted at Lonny. Lonny lifted a spoonful of peas onto his plate and before he could return the spoon, the bowl was gone. Judging the stabs of forks to avoid being pinned to the table, Lonny made a quick grab and secured a biscuit as Ma Landers nodded approval.

The meal was a series of smacks and grunts. Lonny kept his eyes on his plate, squeezed between Washington's jutting elbows on the one side and Shirley beside him on the other. Once and only once during the meal, each of the Landers boys looked up briefly and complimented Ma Landers. "Good, Ma," and that was it.

"Good, Ma," Shirley added.

"Yes ma'am," Lonny nodded. "It sure is. I especially enjoyed the biscuits. Nice and light, that takes some doing. The hard part is gitting them just so and keeping them hot without over—" He halted.

Everybody had stopped eating and they were all staring at him. Lonny smiled, his lips twitching. "Sure is," he said. "Good."

14

Lonny followed the Landers' example when he finished eating. He and Shirley took their plates onto the back porch and raked scraps over the rail to the hounds below. The dogs snarled and fought over the choice tidbits of table food. Ma Landers then sat in a wicker-bottom rocking chair and began sewing by the light of a kerosene lamp, a faint odor of fuel oil filling the room. Everyone else sat around the fireplace on the floor and the Landers boys questioned Lonny about his experiences in Cypress Swamp.

"What did you eat?" Big Bob pressed.

"Caught possums and whatever," Lonny said, truthfully.

"Raw?" Washington asked. "How'd you build a fire?"

"Keep one lit all the time."

"Didn't you hear everyone searching for you?" Morton questioned.

"Sometimes, but I couldn't get to where they were."

Bucky shook his head, impressed. "Ssure iss ssomething!"

"Did you ever see Weakfoot?" Morton asked.

"Never."

"Nobody ever lived that long in Cypress

Swamp afore," Big Bob stated, "excepting maybe old man Smutt."

The name startled Lonny. Ma Landers looked up from her sewing. "Never mind about that," she ordered.

"They ssay—ssome ssay—he'ss living there yet," Bucky added, ignoring Ma Landers' command.

"Couldn't be!" Washington snorted. "He'd be 'gator-ate by now for sure. Twelve, thirteen years it's been since he was last seen."

Ma Landers stood over them. "I want no more talk about that man," Ma said. "No more!"

"Come on, Ma. Tell Lonny about how it happened."

Shirley jumped to her feet. "No! Hush up!"

The brothers laughed and Ma roared for silence. Shirley ran across the room and out the door. Ma saw Lonny's indecision and she jerked her head toward the door. "Git after her, boy," Ma directed. The laughter of the Landers brothers followed Lonny into the dark.

He found Shirley by the creek along the path he would take for home. He stood there, making his presence known, waiting for her to speak. In the bright moonlight, the creek ran pale silver.

"Sit aside me," Shirley beckoned. Lonny did so. They watched the ripples of water, listening to the sound the stream made rushing past their feet. Shirley spoke as though Lonny had asked her about the story Ma Landers wouldn't tell.

"Makes Ma sick to remember," Shirley said softly. "Makes her belly twist and she can't keep food on her stomach just from remembering."

Lonny made no effort to encourage Shirley or stop her.

"Ma had the two brothers and she loved them more than any woman's got a right to love her men, even if they be brothers to her," Shirley related. "Ma adored Tom Smutt and she worshipped Malcolm. They were of a happy home."

Shirley spoke in a flat tone, her words coming as though memorized from listening to the story many times. "When Grandpa died, he left his farm to Tom and Malcolm to share alike. Ma married and moved away. But Landers died—he was Bob, Washington, Bucky, and Morton's pa."

Lonny could feel the girl's tension and as she spoke she rubbed her hands together, the fingers spread and held in such a way that only the palms touched. "Ma came back here then. She lived in a house between Uncle Tom and Uncle Malcolm. The farm was big and Tom Smutt was a good farmer. Fact was, Tom being such a good farmer was part of the hate that began to build in Malcolm. Tom's cotton was always the best grade and he got more bales to the acre. His chickens laid an egg a day even in a molt, so it seemed to Malcolm. Malcolm used to joke about Uncle Tom's cows giving sweeter milk and more cream to a gallon eating the same grass as his cows. Malcolm joked, but he wasn't smiling and when he did his lips turned down like he was hurting at the same time. He was jealous—even Ma said so. Being jealous is bad enough but being jealous so other folks can see it makes the hurt worse. Tom Smutt was the best farmer, that was all there was to it."

Shirley's voice was a drone in the night. "Malcolm and Tom shared profits half and half. Malcolm got half the cotton even if his cotton got the weevils and his tomato plants withered with blight—he got half. Still, they farmed separate and it ate at Malcolm to always be second best to Tom Smutt. Then, the year of the killing, Malcolm raised a field of corn like nobody ever saw in all of ten counties! That corn stood taller and greener and there were more ears to a stalk than folks could ever remember seeing afore. They talked about Malcolm's corn from here to Augusta! Tassels two fingers long hung from the ears. Like a picture in *Progressive Farmer,* was that corn. From sixty miles away people came to see Malcolm's corn and he spent the whole day standing aside the road telling how he come to git such a crop. Folks stopped and admired that corn. They listened to Malcolm like folks had never listened to Malcolm afore."

Shirley's voice trembled a little and rose. "Tom Smutt had his hogs, seventeen or eighteen of them, all prize hogs, penned next to the crop of corn. Two brood sows about to have litters and the rest shoats and butchers goin' to slaughter in the fall."

Lonny wiped his hands down his britches.

"The hogs got out—or was let out," Shirley said, emphasizing her words. "The hogs trampled Malcolm's corn and tore down the stalks and ate the ears. They wrecked his beautiful corn."

Shirley was crying, her voice contorted, and still Lonny did not try to stop her. Shirley said, "Tom was at Ma's. Ma's second husband—my pa—died just a few weeks afore and Tom was over helping Ma the best he could. He took me with him, holding my hand and walking slow. We went down the road, him carrying a shotgun and more or less hunting squirrels. A neighbor came running up and told him Malcolm was shooting Uncle Tom's hogs. At first, Tom didn't believe it and the neighbor had to say it again and again. Tom picked me up and commenced to run all the way to the cornfield, maybe a half mile. I—I don't remember that too clear," she said, as though not to remember was shameful.

"Tom hollered at Malcolm to stop it. Malcolm must of been crazy! He kept shooting those hogs and I can remember it still; hogs know when you aim to kill them. They was screaming and running and Malcolm was shooting them down. Malcolm accused Uncle Tom of turning the hogs in the field of corn on purpose, just to ruin his corn. Tom said Malcolm was lying. Tom picked me up again and started toward home, hissing between his teeth when he breathed. Malcolm commenced screaming dirty words and came charging across the field. He said he was goin' to kill Uncle Tom. Tom told him, quiet like, to watch his tongue. Malcolm reached the fence and said, 'I'm goin' to kill you, Tom!' and Uncle Tom turned to walk away. Malcolm said, 'Put down that baby and turn around or I'll shoot you as you stand!' Uncle Tom put me down aside the road and told me to say there. He turned around and Uncle Malcolm was starting over the fence. He warned Uncle Malcolm not to cross the fence. He said—I remember he said—'Sure's your foot touches ground this side of that fence, I'll kill you Malcolm, brother or no brother.'"

Shirley's sobs were so heavy now, her words came in broken sentences. "Tom told Malcolm twice more and Malcolm said, 'You won't kill me, you ain't got the guts.' Malcolm had his rifle along the top rail holding it with both hands gitting ready to climb over. Tom watched and said again, 'Don't come over the fence, Malcolm,' but Malcolm kept coming. Soon as his legs were over the fence, Malcolm swung his rifle around to jump down and Tom pulled both triggers of his shotgun."

Shirley's cries made Lonny reach for her. She pulled away, turning her back.

"Malcolm sat there shot and dying and he

said to Tom, 'Well," he said, calm as if he was talking about the weather, 'well, you did it.' "

Shirley walked away, leaving Lonny in the dark, saying not a word of parting.

Got to help that old man, Lonny thought. If he's still alive, I got to help him.

The next morning, as the sun rose over Cypress Swamp, Lonny stood at Smutt's old camp-site. The gunnysack lay in shreds and bits of cheesecloth were strewn about. The markings of coon and possum in the black mud left no doubt the goods had gone to animals.

Lonny fashioned a spring trap to frighten any animals that climbed the limb from which a new sack hung. He made a shield of bamboo and cane barbs woven above the vine rope which would cause a possum or coon to fall if the animal tried to climb around it to get to the sack. On limbs around the sack, Lonny hung cane shoots in such a manner that the slightest breeze would knock them together, thus "spooking" most creatures like bear and deer and maybe even the possum and coons for a while.

He stood back and surveyed his work and decided it was well done. To further insure the safety of the sack, he removed a shirt he had worn wrapped around him and had slept with for several nights. He hung the shirt next to the base of the oak. The human odor would keep many would-be thieves away, possibly for several nights. Still, if the sack hung there long enough, the swamp animals would get it.

The following morning, Lonny was back and nothing was changed. He came to the camp only long enough to be sure the sack was still untouched. He came again the next day and still the sack was not molested.

Smutt's bound to be dead, Lonny reprimanded himself. Why waste food and time pretending he ain't?

Several days later he found the sack torn open, the contents scattered here and there as though ravaged by wild animals.

Coons, Lonny decided. Go on now, Bascombe, be a fool and bother to make it hard for them to git again!

Even as he thought the words, Lonny began to secure a fresh sack of food on the limb.

Maybe, he thought defensively, just maybe the old man is playing it smart and he's even got me fooled into thinking he ain't alive. But how about the saucepans?

Lonny searched the area. No sign of the metal utensils. Still, coons might steal something like that just for the curiosity of it. The knife? Where was the knife he had included? No sign of it, either. He was only deluding himself, surely. Too many creatures carried away such things. Crows, coons, always taking things to their nests and dens.

"The old man's dead for sure," Lonny said aloud to Bay as they walked toward home. "But we'll keep coming back a while longer, I reckon."

15

Lonny spent his days watching the sun, waiting for late afternoon when he could go visit Shirley. He found himself thinking of her and acting like a wiggly pup, twisting and fidgeting until time to go over. Of a Sunday, they went to church together and Lonny stood proud, knowing all eyes were on him. The sensation of his experiences had made Lonny Bascombe's story as well known as the tale of old man Smutt's murder of his brother, or Doc Manners and his battle with Weakfoot.

In the mornings, when there was no work to be done and Shirley was busy, Lonny trained Bay. He taught the hound to heel, fetch, and hold. He tied a string to a long pole cut from a cane stand, and to the string a ball stuck through with feathers. Dangling the ball before the hound, Lonny taught Bay to follow the fleet movements of a bird and to fetch when the ball fell to earth like a lifeless bird.

"Goin' to put that hound on birds?" Pa asked.

"I'm goin' to teach him to hunt everything," Lonny said.

"Redbone's not meant to be a bird dog," Pa suggested.

"Might as well try," Lonny reasoned, and Pa admitted it wouldn't hurt to try. When Bay was six months old, he was already learning. Lonny took the pup into the swamp where he taught the hound to search out the scent of coon and possum, dragging the hide of the intended prey before Bay, saying, "Sic, sic—git on it, Bay—git on it."

Every week or two, Lonny carried another sack of supplies to Smutt's former camp. He made periodic searches for the old man but not the first sign did he find.

The coming of winter brought cold nights when the dew crystallized into frost before morning and left the glens in crisp blades of iced sawgrass. Lonny took kerosene then, and two old blankets Aunt Louise had put in the barn for use with new calves that would come in the spring. Always, when Lonny took anything for Smutt, he kept it in hiding and took so little it would not arouse questions from Aunt Louise and Pa. When Lonny next returned to the campsite the kerosene and blankets were gone. For the first time he knew for sure. Smutt still lived.

He knows I'm on to him, Lonny thought, and the game made him smile. That smart old coot! Had me fooled all this time. Don't reckon he could turn down the fuel oil and blankets. Might be he's beginning to trust me.

Lonny looked toward the trackless interior of the swamp. Smutt must have gone deeper than ever into the bayous and lakes to find another, safer haven. Somehow, Smutt had done the impossible and escaped the wrath of the hurricane.

He ain't killable, Lonny mused.

Winter was a time for fixing, Pa said. Lonny and Pa spent their days mending the split-rail fence, repairing harness, and patching things that needed it. Like seeds sleeping under frosted earth, people pulled into their homes these few short cold months. Aunt Louise went to quilting bees, caught up on her sewing, or relaxed and read. Shirley came over almost daily and sat with Aunt Louise, helping and learning at the same time. Lonny cleaned the barn and while he swept the loft, Bay rushed around below chasing an occasional rat that scampered into the open.

A day never passed that Smutt was not on Lonny's mind, for at least a few minutes. Lonny found a pitted, rusty skillet in the barn. It was something Aunt Louise would never consider using again. Remembering the battered pan that Smutt used for his cooking, Lonny spent several afternoons scrubbing the skillet with pumice. It gave him satisfaction knowing that Smutt would appreciate the cast-off item as though it were new!

At Christmas, Lonny dug down into the sock where he kept the money he had earned through the year. There was a quarter he'd gotten for a laying hen he'd sold. A dollar was crumpled around some pennies, which he had earned by helping Mr. Beaudry slaughter hogs last winter. All together, Lonny had nearly three dollars. He spent a dollar each on Aunt Louise and Pa. For Aunt Louise he bought spools of different colored threads and some stainless steel needles. For Pa, Lonny got a box of double-ought shotgun shells. He spent the rest of his money, ninety-two cents, buying a hand axe and hone, which he took out to Smutt.

No matter how long Lonny waited, the sack was left untouched when he was nearby. But when he returned, it was always gone. Hoping to catch a glimpse of the old man, Lonny tried walking away and circling back. What he found made him laugh aloud. Smutt had taken the sack in the time Lonny was gone.

Outsmarted me! Lonny grinned. He's watching for sure.

Then one morning, the sack was still there.

Might be, Smutt forgot what day it is, Lonny thought. But he knew better. The weekly supplies were too important to Smutt. He wouldn't forget.

Could of been busy with a new kill, smoking it, Lonny considered. He left the sack and returned again the next day. It was undisturbed.

"Something's wrong! He'd have come by now," Lonny said, his voice heard only by Bay. The dog cocked his head to one side, trying to make sense of the sounds.

All that afternoon, Lonny did his chores unhappily. He and Pa were throwing rocks into a wagon as the mule snorted impatiently, waiting to pull forward a few more feet.

"Something bothering you, boy?" Pa asked.

"Just thinking, Pa."

Pa nodded. "I reckon a man has to stop talking if he means to do any serious thinking."

Lonny worked, head down and silent, as he considered the things that could happen to a man alone out in Cypress Swamp.

That night, during supper, Lonny shoved food around on his plate, eating little and saying nothing.

"You feel all right, Lonny?" Aunt Louise questioned.

"Just tired, that's all."

"Want some biscuits and gravy?"

"No ma'am, Aunt Louise. I reckon I'll go on to bed. I want to go out looking for a deer stand tomorrow morning."

He was awake for a long time after Pa and Aunt Louise were asleep.

"Let him be all right," Lonny prayed. "He don't deserve to suffer any more than he has."

The sun wasn't up the next morning when Lonny left the house. A knee-deep blanket of thick ground fog shrouded the swamp as boy and dog made their way to the old campsite. When he finally reach the tree, Lonny groaned aloud. The sack was there, untouched.

"Got to be something is wrong!"

For an instant, Lonny debated going to look for the old man. But he hadn't come prepared to stay out here and it might take several days to track Smutt down—if he could track him down.

It was Thursday, and Doc Manners' wagon stood in the backyard, the mule nodding his head and standing easy. When Lonny entered the kitchen, the odor of baking pies tickled his nose. Aunt Louise was molding dough to the proper thickness and placing it in pie tins, ready for filling. Pa and Doc were seated at the table, drinking coffee, talking.

At the first break in the conversation, Lonny spoke. "Pa, I've been thinking about trying to stalk a deer."

"You found a likely spot?" Doc asked.

"I think so. Lots of signs, anyway," Lonny said.

"Whereabouts, son?" Pa asked.

"Cramer Island. Just beyond it."

"Now Lonny," Aunt Louise chided, "you stay away from there. Let's not have you and Weakfoot tangling again."

"With no dog that's not likely to happen," Lonny said. "I was going to work from a blind, so I'll leave Bay home."

"How long will you be gone?" Aunt Louise asked.

"Five, maybe six or seven days."

"A week?" Aunt Louise's voice rose. "No, Lonny, that's too long."

"If you don't bag something the first day or so, you ain't likely to catch anything at all, are you?" Doc asked.

"I got a yen to stay there until I do, though," Lonny said.

"A week's a long time, boy," Pa allowed.

"I can make it all right," Lonny said.

"Lonny," Aunt Louise pleaded softly, "I'd be sick with worry the whole time."

"I did it afore," Lonny replied. "I'll be all right."

They were all looking at him and Lonny could feel his face growing red.

"Lonny," Pa said, "something is wrong here. I can feel it. Want to tell me what it is?

"Please, Pa," Lonny said, almost whispering, "I got to go. I can't talk about it and maybe it's nothing. But I got to go."

Pa was now standing beside him and as he reached for the door, he felt Pa's hand on his arm. Lonny pulled gently and Pa's hand tightened.

"Pa, please."

"Let's talk, son."

Suddenly, Lonny snatched his arm free and bounded out the door, almost knocking Shirley down as she came up the back steps.

"Lonny?" Shirley fussed, then she froze as she saw the look on Pa's face. Lonny raced for the split-rail fence.

"Lonny!" Pa's voice boomed. "Lonny, come back here!"

Stunned, Pa watched the boy scramble over the fence and race across the barren cornfield

toward Cypress Swamp. Pa turned to face Doc
and Aunt Louise. Shirley entered the room without greeting.

"He never stood me down afore," Pa said,
his words choked.

Doc cleared his throat and started to rise
from his chair.

"There's something wrong here," Aunt
Louise said, her eyes wide, a look of fear twisting
her face. "This isn't like Lonny. What could—I
don't understand this at all. He can't be hunting
deer. He didn't take a rifle."

"No food either," Pa said.

Bay stretched and walked out from under the
table. Pa, Doc, Aunt Louise, and Shirley stared
at the dog.

"He never defied me afore," Pa said.

"The boy's growing up," Doc noted gently,
getting ready to take his leave.

"No," Aunt Louise said, firmly. "There's
something wrong."

Pa waved Doc back to the table. "Don't go,
Doc," Pa said. Doc sat again.

"All right," Doc reasoned, "we don't have
to worry about Lonny out there—even with no
food or rifle. The boy knows what he's about.
So, Louise, stop worrying about the boy gitting
'gator-ate or some such."

"He's not goin' hunting," Pa said, his voice
odd.

"No," Doc agreed, "he's not going hunting."

"He said he was," Pa said.

"And he ain't telling the truth," Doc admitted, gruffly.

"What else can he be doing?" Pa questioned.

Embarrassed, Doc did not reply. Shirley
stood by, mute, listening.

Very softly, Aunt Louise said, "I'm afraid."

Then she said again, louder, "Something's wrong. I'm afraid!"

"Now, Louise," Pa said.

"I know something's wrong and you know it too!" Aunt Louise wailed.

She began to cry. "I don't want him lost again. I couldn't stand it. He said he'd be gone a week—"

"Oh!" Shirley gasped.

Aunt Louise stared at the girl. "You know," Aunt Louise said. "You know what it is."

"No—I—" Shirley wiped both hands down her skirt.

"You do know!" Aunt Louise accused.

"I don't really."

But her eyes gave her away, and Shirley could see the adults knew better.

"Where's he goin', girl?" Doc asked.

Shirley shifted uneasily. "I don't know for sure about anything," she blurted.

"Please!" Aunt Louise screamed. "Tell us! For God's sake, Shirley, please!"

"It's Smutt," Shirley whispered. "Lonny's gone looking for Tom Smutt."

"Smutt?" Doc hooted. "Well, good luck to him, then."

Pa's eyes narrowed. "What're you saying, Shirley?"

Shirley's lips quivered and tears rose in her eyes.

"Shirley," Pa demanded, "why did you say that?"

"I followed Lonny," Shirley said, her voice tremulous. "I heard him calling Smutt. Lonny takes bags of food and things and hangs them in a tree, for Smutt. He's been doing it since he came back during the storm."

"Did Lonny tell you this?" Pa said.

"No. I never let on I followed him but the one time, because he was mad. He lied then, telling me he was saying *mutt*, calling his dog. But he didn't have his dog with him."

Pa stared at Doc. "Could it be?"

"I don't know," Doc said. "Twelve, thirteen years it's been." His tone plainly said he didn't believe it.

Aunt Louise stood statue-still, dumbstruck, staring at space.

"How often did Lonny do that?" Pa questioned Shirley.

"Most every week."

"Thirteen years out there," Doc said, "he'd be crazy by now. Crazy as a coon drunk on persimmon wine." Doc's eyes darted back and forth across Pa's face. "It'd be a miracle, if it was true, just to have stayed alive! Skeeter swarms," Doc spoke almost to himself, "fever water, moccasins and chiggers—it'd be a miracle. It can't be true."

Aunt Louise still stared at nothing, her voice sounded distant. "That's where he was all that time. That's why Lonny stayed gone. Smutt had him. It was Smutt keeping Lonny."

"I tell you, no man could survive out there so long," Doc grumbled.

"Lonny did it!" Aunt Louise insisted.

"The boy must've been baiting traps, Louise. Shirley misunderstood what he was doing."

"Lonny took tools and pans, not just food," Shirley said.

Doc faced Pa, his face drawn. "Smutt would be crazy by now. Have to be. Could be—he could be dangerous."

"Oh my God," Aunt Louise cried. "Oh my God, please! Don't let anything happen to my boy!"

"Fix us some food, Louise," Pa said, "we're goin' after him." Pa was already checking his shotgun and rifle.

"Where would he git clothing?" Doc asked nobody in particular. "Or medicine when he got sick? Out like that, anything might kill a man."

Aunt Louise quickly wrapped cheese, biscuits, and a couple of slabs of pork in oilcloth, putting it in a sack with a tin of coffee and a few utensils.

"He'd have to live like an animal," Doc argued.

"Food would be the first and last chore every day, just gitting food enough to stay alive."

"I didn't want to tell on Lonny," Shirley said, speaking quietly, standing next to Aunt Louise.

"You did right, child," Aunt Louise said. Then, glancing at the girl, Aunt Louise halted her work and took Shirley in her arms. "He'll understand," Aunt Louise said. "He'll understand, Shirley. Don't worry. You did right."

Pa turned from the gun rack and spoke to Doc. "You coming?"

"You know good and well I am," Doc snorted.

Shirley ran for the door. "I'll git my brothers!"

"Shirley, no!" Pa called. But she was gone, running for home. At last, she could tell Ma—Tom Smutt was alive!

16

Standing in one of pa's flat-bottomed boats, Lonny poled the craft toward Cramer Island. He would need the food he'd left for Smutt. Cutting down the sack, Lonny returned to the boat and shoved it away from the river bank. He had already considered the places where he might find the old man and now, with deliberate speed, he pushed the boat along using the long pole to propel himself.

There was no point in looking where it was marshy—Smutt would avoid those places. He would not be far from high ground either, so he could trap birds and possums. Lonny had carefully recalled the needs of the old man, the camp he had had before, and what areas might be much the same. He had climbed a towering pine and made mental notes of what he saw. He was looking for the largest isolated island-like spot where an oak would stand above the surrounding scrubland. He saw several. It was toward one of these that he now made his way.

To keep from becoming hopelessly lost, Lonny unraveled the coarse gunnysack, separating the burlap into thick threads. He halted at every turn and tied a thread to a low hanging limb. To a keen eye, the threads were an obvious sign, out of place in the swamp.

Lonny had searched four areas, finding nothing. As he backtracked, he took down his threads so he would not end up confused, with threads branching off this way and that. Taking a new direction, he used the same twine to mark the trail anew. Deeper and deeper into the swamp he was going, and the immense and silent area closed around him as he passed, perhaps seeing things no other living man had ever seen.

He spent the first night on a broad, sandy stretch of the river bank, keeping his fire banked low and huddling over it to keep warm. He had made a lean-to for the colder hours and beneath this he slept uncomfortably. Only once did he get out, to keep the fire alive and to climb a tree, looking for any signs of human life in the dark. This he saw, far behind him, and he realized Pa was following him. Lonny correctly guessed there were others too, judging by the glow in the night from several fires. Probably Doc Manners and the Landers boys, Lonny decided. Grimly, he realized their penetration into the swamp might spook Smutt and drive him deeper under cover. All Lonny could hope to do was to stay far enough ahead to surprise the old man.

As soon as the chilled fog cover lifted, Lonny climbed the tallest tree he could find, searching out the particular stands of oak he was seeking. Then, back in his boat and using instinct as his guide, he poled farther into the swamp.

The swamp by winter was not the same noisy place it was in spring, summer, and fall. At this time of year, the 'gators and other reptiles had taken to their burrows. The birds went about the business of hunting food, almost always mute. Bear, deer, bobcats, and other large animals generally moved in the early and late hours of day. Rounding a curve in the sluggish river, Lonny surprised a stand of fifteen or twenty deer getting water on a nearby bank. The deer, poised for flight, looked at him and seemed as surprised to see Lonny as he was at seeing so many deer in one place.

How deep he had gone, how far he was from home, Lonny had no way of knowing. The second night out, he seriously considered returning. He was unhappy with himself for not handling the matter with Pa better than he had. He knew that Aunt Louise was worrying about him. But he had come this far and he decided to keep looking, at least for a few more days.

During the day, Pa and the others had gained on Lonny as the boy wandered up one stream and then another, carefully crossing and recrossing the same path, going from one bayou to another. Pa had surely found the strings by now and this was speeding their approach. But Lonny dared not skip tying the threads—otherwise he might end up hopelessly confused and totally lost.

It was the fourth day out when Lonny discovered a huge, mirror-smooth lake surrounded on three sides by massive stands of cypress trees. On the far side of the lake stood a tremendous oak, with a lesser oak close behind it. Even before he moved into the lake, Lonny knew this would be it. There was no way to approach the oak by water and not be seen. Lonny considered beaching his boat and taking the marshy, quicksand-filled bogs behind the cypress trees around the lake, but the way would be hard and risky. He pushed his boat toward the center of the lake. If Smutt saw him and ran, so be it. At least, Lonny would know the old man was alive and well enough to escape.

The shoreline was sheltered by a stand of

water grass. When he reached it, Lonny jumped from his boat, pushing through cattails and shouting, "Smutt!"

Under the oak, propped against the trunk of the tree, Smutt looked up at him. The old man's face was swollen, his right cheek badly scratched.

"Smutt," Lonny said, kneeling beside the old man, "what happened?"

Smutt's breathing came shallow, quick.

"Weakfoot," the old man gasped. "Tried to steal my deer—smoked deer."

Lonny looked down the man's body, and the boy's stomach knotted sickly.

"When did it happen?" Lonny asked.

"Week—maybe two—ago." Smutt swallowed several times. "Fire went out. Couldn't keep it proper. Couldn't git wood."

"I'll build another one," Lonny said, his voice trembling. He tried to keep his eyes off the old man's wounds, but he couldn't.

By the time Lonny had built a new fire, Smutt was babbling feverishly. Lonny did what he could to cleanse the old man's arms, legs, and stomach, and the effort made him cry with frustration. Each scratch was infected.

"Pa!" Lonny screamed.

"Pa . . . Pa . . . Pa. . . ." The echo rippled away.

"Pa!" Lonny yelled again. "Hurry!"

His yells aroused Smutt and the old man's eyes darted here and there with some of the wariness Lonny was accustomed to seeing. Then Smutt's yellow eyes wavered and closed. He was unconscious again.

His hands shaking, Lonny heated water, searching all the while for food he could prepare that Smutt might be able to eat in his condition.

"Please, Pa," Lonny whispered, "please hurry."

Using warm water and a sliver of soap that remained, Lonny bathed the old man's wounds. Deadly gangrene infested them all.

"I got to take you back, Smutt," Lonny said.

"No."

Lonny looked the old man in the eye. "You goin' to die, Smutt. Unless I git you to a doctor quick, you goin' to die."

Smutt grunted. "Goin'—die—anyhow," he rasped.

"Maybe not, if we git a doctor," Lonny said, wincing as he touched a tender area which made Smutt cry aloud.

"I hoped—you'd come—boy."

"I'm here," Lonny said, simply.

"Hand to paw, boy," Smutt related. "Fought that big he cat—hand—to paw."

Lonny nodded.

"Stabbed him bad—like to have kilt him—but he got away. Caught that cat—stealing my smoked —deer."

"Smutt, I'm goin' to carry you to the boat," Lonny declared.

Smutt twisted violently and shouted, "No! I ain't goin'!"

Lonny's face showed his feelings. Smutt was dying, why fight with him over it? Tears trickled down Lonny's cheeks.

"Fix us some—sassafras—"

Lonny stirred the fire and placed a saucepan in the embers. He found the sassafras roots and was about to drop them in to boil when Smutt called.

"Oh!" Smutt cried. "Forgot! There's coffee."

Lonny discarded the sassafras and poured coffee grounds in the water instead.

Smutt stared straight ahead, eyes glazed.

"Hand to paw," Smutt recalled. "Fought Weakfoot, hand to paw. He bit me—I bit him. I bit his ear off." Smutt began coughing and didn't stop until he was spent.

"Tried chase Weakfoot—into quicksand. Too smart. Too smart, that cat. Cornered him—he—had to fight."

Lonny squatted beside the old man, holding Smutt's hand. "Never corner a cat—never," Smutt warned. "Jumped me—I—stabbed him three—" Smutt held up three fingers. "A cat's got no holding place, boy. If his teeth don't git you, his claws do." Smutt paused, breathing hard.

"Boy?"

"Yes sir?"

"You only man—ever good—really good—to old Smutt."

Tears surged in Lonny's eyes.

"Brought old Smutt—food, salt." The old man's eyes brightened. "Eggs! Found the eggs!"

"I figured you'd like eggs," Lonny choked.

"Good eggs," Smutt whispered. "Yore good boy."

"Smutt, please let me take you to a doctor. You got to be hurting. He can stop that."

Smutt snorted. "I ain't goin' back, boy. Don't want to go back."

"Yes you do!" Lonny insisted. "You can sleep on a bed again and eat hot food. No more worrying about mosquitoes and gnats. Git to drink all the well water you want."

Smutt smiled and Lonny knew the old man was only half listening. "Fought that cat—big he cat—"

The old man's eyes closed and for a terrifying moment, Lonny thought Smutt had died.

Please. Don't let him die.

The coffee was boiling. Lonny removed his hand from Smutt's gnarled fingers and poured himself a cup. He couldn't find the sugar. Then he discovered a log hollowed out and filled with syrup boiled down from sugar. He dug some out with one finger and raked it into his cup. Smutt lay, eyes closed, breathing easier. Lonny walked over the camp area. Dried blood flecks showed where Smutt's fight with the panther had taken place, at the edge of a quicksand mire.

Lonny found a few tracks in the moist river bank, showing where the cat had run, leaving spatters of blood on the bushes. That cat would be easy to track now, Lonny thought. He hoped somebody would bring their dogs, but he doubted it would happen. He debated how long it would take Pa to get here.

Lonny built up the fire. He went into a wooded area nearby, stepping carefully, watching for snakes in the coming dark. He broke off pine limbs and tore up a rotted cypress bole, cutting it with the axe he had given Smutt. The fire became a roaring blaze that lighted the entire camp. In case Pa did come in the dark, they'd be able to find him.

Lonny decided not to try and move the old man to the lean-to. He got one of the blankets and, dirty as it was, spread it next to Smutt. Lonny stretched out beside the old man. Lying on his side, his eyes on Smutt's bare chest and the old man's face in the firelight, Lonny watched the movements that proved life. Sometime after the moon was high, Lonny fell asleep listening to the labored breathing of the injured man.

The low moaning call of a cow horn awoke Lonny. He sat up immediately.

"Smutt!"

The old man was gone. Lonny heard the cow horn again and threw back his head, cupping his hands: "Hoy, hoy, hoy!" His voice caromed over Cypress Swamp and birds rose from trees surrounding the camp, their wings a flurry of sound.

"Hoy, hoy, hoy!" Lonny cried again.

"Oy . . . oy . . . oy," his voice came back to him. The cow horn blew again, three short, sharp blasts.

Lonny wheeled, looking for the old man. He saw where Smutt had dragged himself, clawing the soft earth. Following the signs, Lonny pushed through a palmetto thicket.

"Smutt! What are you doing, old man?"

Smutt sat in the center of a quicksand pool and Lonny could see the old man was straddling a sunken log.

"I heard men," Smutt said. "Coming for me."

Lonny stepped carefully, moving toward the old man.

"Don't come," Smutt warned. "Not but one way here."

"Come on, Smutt," Lonny implored. "Come back."

"No." The old man supported himself with both hands, up to his armpits in the mire, his wounds filled with sand and dirt.

"I ain't aiming to go back," Smutt explained.

Lonny heard Pa and Doc shouting to him. "Over here, Pa!" Lonny yelled. Then, to Smutt, "You aim to sit there and suffer, maybe days?"

Smutt glanced at Pa and Doc as they came beside the boy. "No, I don't," Smutt said.

The Landers brothers joined them, testing the ground gingerly, then stopping at the edge of the mire. Lonny heard Big Bob tell someone to get a rope.

"Hold on, old man," Big Bob said. "We'll throw you a rope. You can tie it around—"

"I don't need—don't need a rope."

"All right," Pa agreed. "I'll come out and carry you back."

"Don't want—to go back." Smutt leaned slowly to one side. Smiling all the while as the men watched him, the old man fell sideways into the mire.

"Smutt!" Lonny yelled. "No! Wait!"

Lonny lunged forward and Pa grabbed the boy.

"Don't do it, Smutt!" Lonny begged. The old man did not move and therefore sank slowly.

"Throw him a rope," Big Bob commanded. One of the others threw a rope and it fell across Smutt's shoulder. The old man did not so much as look at it.

"Grab the rope, Smutt," Doc Manners urged.

Everyone chorused, "Grab the rope. Grab the rope!"

Smutt kept smiling. His beard lay atop the mire and he was now chest-deep.

"Boy—"

Lonny was crying openly, Pa holding him.

"Boy—you good—good man—boy. Make old Smutt—happy. Smutt's friend."

"If you're a friend of mine," Lonny begged, "grab the rope!"

Smutt's smile faded and he stared at Lonny with a sadness that made everyone hold still, saying nothing.

"I ain't one of you, boy. Smutt's—like—Weakfoot. A animal—both us."

They watched, helpless to aid the man who wanted no help. Lonny tried again to go out to the submerged log and Pa held him back. Smutt was all under except his head and beard. The rope lay atop the quicksand where his shoulder sank.

"Fought that—cat—hand—to paw."

"Pa! Please, we got to help him!"

Smutt tilted back his head to keep his mouth out of the mud. "Fought hand—to—paw." He closed his lips and gasped air through his nose. He breathed quickly and almost desperately took a final breath and closed his eyes tightly. Only his hair and the tip of his beard showed above the bog.

"Oh, no! No!" Lonny sank to his knees, covering his face.

They stood there waiting, but the old man never reached for the rope. The men looked at one another. Big Bob walked around the camp picking up a pot here and a fork there, looking at them. He inspected the lean-to and the place where the cat and Smutt had fought. Then they all got into their boats, Lonny's sobs the only sound other than the poles slipping water. Pa shoved off and they headed for home.

Somewhere up ahead, Lonny heard Doc Manners say, "Best thing, most likely. Crazy of course. Been out here so long he was bound to be."

"Never would've believed it, if I hadn't seen him," Big Bob said.

"Crazy," Doc replied.

"He wasn't crazy!" Lonny shouted.

The outburst halted conversation.

Lonny looked up and found Pa poling the boat, his face troubled.

"He wasn't crazy, Pa."

"All right, Lonny."

"Pa?"

"Yes, boy?"

"He kept me a prisoner a long time. Then—

then he brought me home in the storm because I was sick. He saved my life."

After a long silence, Lonny added, "I'm sorry, Pa."

Pa's hand gripped Lonny's shoulder for a moment, then returned to pushing their boat.

That cat did it . . . goin' to git that cat . . . git that cat. . . .

17

For weeks, people discussed nothing but Smutt. Awed, disbelieving, they marveled that any man could or would suffer such loneliness and hardship. There were even those who flatly denied it could have happened. With the passing of time, the panther wounded by Tom Smutt became more the topic of conversation. Smutt was gone. Weakfoot was very much alive. Every isolated farm section around Cypress Swamp was losing calves, pigs, and fowl. Forced by its wounds to take easy prey, the panther was now a threat to any person who might stand in the way of escape. One farmer after another claimed he had shot at, and missed, the panther. The men banded together with packs of dogs and rifles. Each hunt was wasted. The panther stayed clear of the hounds and survived.

"You goin' hunting Weakfoot?" Bucky Landers asked Lonny hopefully.

"First chance I git," Lonny said. But he felt an ache in his stomach every time the cat came to mind. He was haunted by Smutt's dying words, "Smutt's like Weakfoot—a animal—both us."

Lonny saw that as truth. Smutt had been driven to the swamp, living like a wild animal to stay alive. He had spent all of every day laboring for one thing—food for tomorrow. So it was with

Weakfoot, Lonny thought. Man hurt the panther. Now man paid the price. The cat had no choice but to take barnyard creatures.

As much as Lonny had once wanted the death of Weakfoot, strangely, he now felt a certain admiration for the beast. It was almost as if Smutt and Weakfoot had become one creature now that Smutt was gone. Lonny almost hoped the big cat would go on living. Yet at the same time, remembering how Weakfoot had killed both Smutt and Bay, Lonny wanted more than ever to get the panther once and for all.

"Mind if I go down to Millpond with Shirley?" Lonny asked Aunt Louise one evening. Shirley sat on the backsteps, waiting.

"Don't be too late," Aunt Louise replied.

"With Weakfoot out stealing shoats and young calves," Pa suggested, "you best take a rifle and Bay."

Lonny disappeared into the bedroom, looking for a comb. He took so long Pa called, "Something you best learn, boy—don't keep a girl waiting longer than it takes a firefly to douse his light."

Grinning, Lonny paused to take down Pa's rifle and put several shells in his pocket. Bay scrambled up from the floor where he'd been snoozing, anticipating some night hunting.

Together, Lonny, Shirley, and Bay walked slowly toward Millpond.

"Seems all I hear these days is Lonny Bascombe's name," Shirley said. "Wednesday night prayer meeting at church, all they talked about was you."

"Tales grow with the telling of them," Lonny noted.

"Sure must," Shirley laughed. "To hear some of them, you'd think Lonny Bascombe was the Daniel Boone of this county! I reckon it makes exciting thinking and that's how come people tend to stretch things a bit."

"I reckon that's natural," Lonny said. He really enjoyed it, although he wouldn't admit it to anyone. But now he better understood why Doc Manners always hushed when folks told about the time Doc and Weakfoot fought. Chances were, the stories were even more exciting than the truth and Doc felt it wouldn't hurt to hold his tongue and let them talk.

They sat on a bridge rail, listening to water falling over a wooden dam that held back the millpond lake. Lonny made sure his weapon was unloaded and leaned it against the bridge. Bay went off through the woods sniffing out scents. Shirley reached over and took Lonny's hand.

"Lonny?"

"What?"

"I— like you very much."

"I like you," he said, and winced at the hollow sound of it. "I like you very much," he added. He tried to think of something to say and thinking of nothing worth saying, remained silent, holding her hand, conscious of the perspiration between their palms.

Bay came into the lane and stood at Lonny's side, panting from his run.

"What was that?" Shirley asked.

"What?"

"That sound."

Lonny listened. "I don't hear anything."

Bay's hair bristled so sharply Lonny heard it crackle. The dog growled and Lonny reached down and took Bay by the collar.

"Did you hear it then?" Shirley asked, her voice strained.

"No. What was it?"

Then he heard it. The squeal of a pig scared

half to death. It came from the Landerses' land. A shout carried in the still night air, and the roar of a shotgun made Bay struggle to get free.

"Hold on, Bay! Bay!"

Another shot and more shouting.

Bay wiggled so fiercely Lonny had to hold the dog with both arms.

"Lonny!"

Shirley's scream brought Lonny to a standing position. Through the night the dark form of a loping animal ran down the lane toward them, barely visible in the patches of moonlight that filtered through the overhanging trees. Bay broke loose and Lonny sprawled forward, trying to grab the hound. He heard Shirley scream, "Weakfoot!"

The hound and cat met at full run. Bay yelped as the mighty panther slashed with claws that could rake open a dog with a single swipe.

"Bay!" Lonny grabbed his rifle and jammed a shell into the chamber. The hissing, spitting cat was a blur in the dark. Bay circled the panther, darting in and out, snapping, snarling.

"Bay! Stand still!" The hound was too excited to hear. "Fool dog! *Bay!*" he screamed.

Lonny ran forward, closing on the cat.

"Lonny, be careful!"

In an instant, the cat's back was turned and Lonny took three steps closer. He aimed the rifle and Bay charged the beast in the same moment. Lonny jerked up the barrel just as his finger pulled the trigger. The explosion directly overhead made the panther whirl. The cat reared back, claws slashing. Lonny's legs were knocked from beneath him. The panther charged the boy and Bay lunged and seized the cat by the neck. Dog and beast rolled over and over as Lonny scrambled away.

Bay wailed and the cat broke, bounding

blindly toward Shirley. Lonny swung his weapon as he would a club. The rifle struck the cat broadside. The panther paused, stunned. Bay was at the cat before Lonny could reload. With a mighty blow, the panther bowled Bay aside and was off and running with Bay close behind, the hound's voice tolling the call of the chase. Lonny shoved another shell into the rifle.

"Call Pa!" Lonny demanded. "I'm goin' after Bay."

Shirley grabbed his arm. "No! You got no lantern! Please don't go."

Lonny removed her hand from his arm. "I ain't goin' to lose another hound to that cat," he vowed.

He raced after the yelping dog. He could only guess at the terrain in the moonlight. His shoes sucked in moist earth and filled with mud and water. Briars snatched his clothing and tore his face and hands. He ran blind, bumping stumps and knocking into raised cypress knees. Ahead, running faster and surer than Lonny, the panther raced from the dreaded hound, the cat's stride broken by the stab wounds caused by Smutt's knife. The hound caught the cat, and lightning fast the panther whirled to sink its fangs into Bay's shoulder. But as the weakened beast turned, Bay ran headlong into the cat and they rolled end over end, the panther's claws slashing viciously. Lonny crashed through the underbrush. From the black shadows came the sounds of combat.

"Bay! Here!"

The panther and Bay were locked in mortal battle and the hound knew only what was at hand. Lonny pushed nearer, eyes wide, straining to see.

The panther smelled man and exerted the greatest effort possible to throw off the hound. Twisting from its back to gain its feet, the beast lunged away and fell, the man-made wounds now taking their toll. Immediately, Bay was on the cat's back.

Lonny threw himself at tangled vines, led only by the guttural sounds of snarling animals. He knew one fact: given long enough, the panther would slay Bay. Lonny drove himself at the wall of vines and undergrowth.

Pa's voice came through the darkness, calling. "Here! Pa! Over here!"

Light. He had to have light. The thought of facing Weakfoot in total dark brought a terror to Lonny that made his legs go weak. But then, fiercely, he told himself, I lost one dog with my being a coward. Better hurt than shamed the rest of my life! With that he assaulted the vegetation holding him back.

The cat fought frantically and suddenly tore free. Filled with panic the panther jumped and struck Lonny, knocking the boy backward. Bay leaped across Lonny and the boy cried out in anger and frustration. Several of the Landers' hounds ran past in the dark joining Bay in pursuit of the panther. Lonny ran after the pack.

The roar of Pa's rifle brought Lonny to a momentary halt. Then harder than ever he ran. The light of Pa's lantern showed the way. The hounds were there, the snarling, growling, yelping cries telling Lonny of the scene even before he saw it. Lonny broke into the glen where cat, Pa, and hounds had met. He stopped, aghast.

Boiling black and red, the hounds and panther rolled. One of the Landers' dogs lay dying. Pa looked down to load another cartridge in his rifle and in that split-second the cat shook off the last hound. As though sensing his advantage, the panther made a giant leap and covered half the distance between the dogs and Pa.

"Look out!" Lonny screamed.

Pa's head jerked up as the crazed cat in mid-air came down on him. The panther's front paws went over Pa's shoulders and the claws sank into his back.

"The hind feet! Pa! Grab his hind feet!"

Pa's powerful hands closed over the panther's rear legs and held away the deadly, razor-sharp claws from his chest and stomach. With a sudden twist, Pa threw the black cat off and the hounds were on it. Lonny lifted his rifle, aimed at a spot beneath the dogs, and squeezed the trigger.

The cat jerked so violently under the impact of the bullet the dogs were thrown aside. The wounded beast made a desperate dash for a tree, stumbled, and went down under the hounds again. Pa stood transfixed. Lonny ran forward to insure the accuracy of the next shot. He stood over the fighting animals and looked down on the panther, the cat on its back, claws spread, mouth frothing. Dimly, Lonny realized the cat raked his leg. He jabbed the rifle against the cat's chest and pulled the trigger. With the explosion of the rifle, the panther leaped straight up, flipped, and fell back. The hounds tore at the black body.

Lonny stood looking at the scene, scarcely able to believe it was all over and the panther was dead. The shadows cast by the hounds in the light of the lantern danced eerily beyond the deliriously victorious dogs. Slowly, Lonny turned and faced Pa. Morton and Washington Landers stood at the edge of the glen, stunned by what they had witnessed. Pa stood as motionless as a stump, his eyes glazed from the shock of the cat's attack.

"Pa?" Lonny said, uncertainly.

"Best git the dogs, son," Pa said, finally.

The Landers brothers pulled the hounds away from the still form of the cat. Washington and

Morton dragged the dogs to a tree and tied them, and the hounds lay foaming at the mouth, panting. Then, with the lantern, they examined Pa's back. Four deep blue punctures showed where the cat's claws had found a hold. Bucky and Big Bob came crashing through the underbrush and halted, mute, when they realized what had happened.

"You made me proud tonight, Lonny," Pa said, his voice quavering.

"You got more courage than me," Morton Landers said.

"No I don't," Lonny said, sharply. Then to Pa, "I was scared, Pa. Terribly scared. I was scared the first time I met Weakfoot and it was my being so cowardly that caused the first Bay to be killed. I shook so hard I couldn't reload and while I was fumbling, Weakfoot killed my dog."

His confession made, Lonny stood silent, head down.

"I was *sure* scared," Pa admitted. "I looked up and saw that cat coming—scared before that, even."

"I reckon Doc Manners would be ashamed of us," Lonny said, his voice husky.

"No cause to be ashamed of fear, boy," Pa said, pulling on his shirt again, shivering like he was cold. "Doc's been hunting that cat for years, just to prove to hisself he ain't scared."

Pa put a shaking hand on Lonny's shoulder. "It took some guts to run that cat with no lantern. Plain guts."

"Sure did," Morton Landers agreed.

Pa gazed at the dead beast. "Weakfoot was brave too. If we had a single hound that fought as hard, we'd be proud." Pa took a deep breath and it caught in his throat like he'd been crying. "Sometimes a man is hard put to tell whether he's brave, or a fool. I think every man wonders whether he's a coward who did the right thing at the right time, or just plain dumb and lucky. I don't expect many brave men honestly know which they are."

Pa sighed, his breath jerking as he did so. "That cat was born natural and died unnatural because of man. The really disgusting thing is, people sometimes do the same thing to one another. Like Smutt."

The Landers brothers helped skin the panther. "Biggest tomcat I ever saw," Washington said.

Big Bob rolled the pelt and handed it to Lonny.

"I reckon it's only right to share half the bounty with y'all," Lonny suggested to the Landers boys. "That'd be a hundred dollars for your share. Hadn't been for your dogs showing up, mine would be dead. You lost a hound. It's only right."

Big Bob extended a hand. "Thanks, Lonny."

Soberly, each of the Landers brothers did the same.

"Maybe we could come over tomorrow, to see the skin by the light of day," Big Bob said. "I mean, if it's all right."

"We'd be obliged to have you," Lonny said.

They turned toward home, the Landers brothers with their dogs, Bay trailing Pa and Lonny. Pa walked as though his back was stiff.

"No, there's no shame to being afraid," Pa stated, as if Lonny had brought up the subject again. "There just ain't no way to measure what's brave. Smutt was brave. He faced death every day all those years out in the swamp. But he ran away and lived that way to escape his punishment, so he was also a coward. After Smutt ran, staying away became the most important thing in his life. Was he brave? Or a coward?"

Lonny thought on it.

Pa spoke as though to himself. Doc Manners once told me about a stage actor who got scared every time he had to give a show. Doc said the actor claimed that being scared helped him give a better show. I reckon being afraid is as natural as being sad, or happy, or crying or laughing. I was scared, let me tell you. That cat around my neck. Plenty scared."

Pa was trembling so hard now, Lonny could see the lantern jiggling in his hand. He took a quick step to get beside Pa, and took the older man's arm. Lonny recognized shock, a freezing of the nerves that could kill a man, Doc called it. Doc once said, shock was like the body was ready to die and when it didn't happen it had to get used to living all over again.

"Pa," Lonny declared, "I love you."

Pa stopped and stared at Lonny. "Seems to me," Pa said softly, "I don't recollect you ever saying that to me afore."

Lonny studied Pa's face. "It did sound funny."

"Not funny," Pa allowed. "I'm proud to hear you say it. There are times when it needs to be put to words."

18

It was hard to realize that almost half a year had
elapsed since Smutt's death. Lonny thought about
the old man often. During those hours alone, his
hands busy with chores, Lonny's mind touched on
his experiences, considering what had happened,
why it happened. The desire to return to Smutt's
camp had grown from a fleeting urge to a daily
debate with himself until, finally, he decided to go.
The nightmares he'd had after the old man died
no longer came upon him. He no longer awoke in
the middle of the night crying aloud.

"You're growing up, that's all," Shirley
allowed, when Lonny discussed it with her. Maybe
learning how *not* to think about something was
as important as learning *how* to think about something else.

Shirley was right. Lonny told himself it was
childlike to want to go back to Smutt's camp.
Nonetheless, he wanted to go. He finished his
breakfast and took down the new rifle Pa had
given him on his birthday. Bay perked his ears
and wagged his tail expectantly.

"That rifle shoot true?" Pa asked.

"Yes sir. That it does."

Aunt Louise wrapped biscuits with smoked
sausage and gave them to Lonny. "No need me

worrying about whether you're goin' to starve all day," she explained. "You won't be back afore sundown, knowing you."

Lonny filled both pockets with cartridges.

"Boy," Pa disapproved, "you take enough shells to start a war when you go hunting."

"Aim to reset my sights," Lonny said. He stopped at the door. "Pa, I'm goin' out to Smutt's old campsite."

After a heavy silence, Pa said, "Be careful."

"I will."

Bay scooted under the fence and Lonny vaulted it with one hand on the rail. They stopped by the Landers house to pick up Shirley. He'd promised to take her with him. Together, they got Lonny's boat into the river.

"Git in," Lonny commanded his dog, pushing off from the bank as Shirley sat forward, both hands on the sides of the craft, smiling. Bay eased around her until he stood up front, forefeet on the leading edge of the boat, peering ahead. The hound yelped foolishly at birds on wing and waving sawgrass. A squirrel flicked his tail rapidly, chattering an angry reply as the boy, girl, and dog passed below. From shallows near a canebrake, a crane rose heavily, then soared low and wide, skimming the surface of the water with the tips of its wings now and then. Lonny dragged his pole to allow a water moccasin to swim across their path without colliding with the craft. Bay snapped at the snake, sending the reptile into a shallow dive.

"You best keep your nose high," Lonny warned the dog, "else you may draw back snake-bit."

"It's very nice out here," Shirley commented as they went deeper into the swamp. "It's peaceful and quiet."

Lonny picked a water hyacinth and gave it to her. Shirley sat holding the blossom in one hand, looking at him, at the river, at the passing banks, grinning.

Reeds still sheltered Smutt's camp from view. Lonny jumped into the lake and dragged the boat toward land. Bay leaped overboard too, floundering and snorting as he paddled to shore. The campsite had yielded to spring rains and summer heat, producing new growth that had crept as close to Smutt's camp as the shade of the oak would allow. The lean-to was down. Ants had infested the old man's syrup log, making the larder their home.

Lonny found a saucepan half-buried in sand. He brushed it clean and placed it beside the remains of the lean-to. Near the water's edge he discovered Smutt's rusting axe, the blade black and corroded.

Ash and charred wood left from fires Smutt had burned were a dirty sore in the sand.

"Where did it happen?" Shirley asked.

"Quicksand," Lonny replied, leading the way. He parted the brush for her, shoving it down with his feet so the weeds would not brush against her. Carefully, because quicksand bogs often floated to new positions, Lonny felt the earth before advancing toward the area.

"There," he said, pointing at the approximate place where Smutt had died.

Silently, Shirley looked at the placid surface. Then she tossed her hyacinth lily onto the mire. Her head dropped and her eyes closed. Lonny did not disturb her until she spoke again.

"He was a good man, Lonny?" she asked, her voice strange. "Or was he bad?"

Lonny considered the question carefully before trying to answer. Then he said, "Good folks

do bad things now and again. Bad folks do good
things now and again. I reckon Smutt was like
Weakfoot. He was bad, or not bad, depending on
what he did to you."

Shirley nodded, an odd expression in her eyes.
"I think he was a good man, then. I used to dream
about him coming to see me at night, when everybody was asleep. I dreamed it when I was awake,
I mean. I dreamed that he would bring me things
he made out of natural wood and he'd tell me
stories through my bedroom window. I had him
all made up in my mind. I saw him as a good man
who did a bad thing. That's the way I like to think
about him."

"That's a good way to think," Lonny agreed.

A breeze stirred the oaks and the leaves
whispered, sighing, as though the massive trees
also agreed with Shirley.

"Well, old man," Lonny said aloud, "I ain't
goin' to come back anymore."

Shirley stood looking at the lily on the mire,
her face blank. Her hand was on Lonny's arm.
They stood there unspeaking for a long time until
Lonny spoke again. "Well, old man, here's good-
bye."

Lonny whistled up Bay and the three of them
shoved off from the bank. The hound, tired of
doing nothing, put his head down and closed his
eyes. Lonny leaned against the pole and pushed
them toward the middle of the lake.

"Thank you for bringing me," Shirley said.

Lonny nodded, then smiled. "I know a good
place for a picnic," he said. "Plenty of shade and
no ants because it's surrounded by water all the
time and underwater part of the year."

"Good! I'm hungry!"

"Me too," Lonny grinned.

Smutt's camp fell away behind them. As they

floated along, laughing, talking the talk of two happy people, Lonny and Shirley did not see the three black heads that raised, listened, and watched. Yellow eyes, young and filled with curiosity, saw the boy, girl, and sleeping dog. Once the boat was beyond the river bend, the young panthers looked about for their mother. She had walked off without them.

They were old enough now, Weakfoot knew, to take care of themselves.

Epilogue

I closed my notebook and sat back. The old man was staring across the yard toward a grove of trees shrouded in Spanish moss.

"To this day," he said, "with automobiles and highways and airplanes that fly so high we can't hear them, I still listen to the sounds from Cypress Swamp."

"What kind of sounds?"

"Long, drawn sighs, then a coughing. Like a big cat. You reckon it could be a great-great-great grandson of Weakfoot?"

"I suppose it could be," I said.

"That'd be a comfort to me. To think we out-lasted them all."

"What part of the story were you?" I asked. He rocked back and forth, smiling. "Old man, were you part of the story?"

He didn't seem to hear me.

ABOUT THE AUTHOR

LINDA CLINE is well qualified to write a book in which the animal characters are as important as the people. She is the president of Land Alive of America, Inc., and has lectured widely on various species, using live animals to illustrate her talks. Southern Georgia provides the setting for *The Ghost of Cramer's Island*, Linda Cline's first novel. A resident of Mobile, Alabama, she is the mother of four children, and is married to novelist Terry Cline, author of *Damon*.